P9-BZR-086

ROBOT RAMPAGE

A BUZZ BEAKER BRAINSTORM

Librarian Reviewer
Laurie K. Holland
Media Specialist (National Board Certified), Edina, MN
MA in Elementary Education, Minnesota State University, Mankato

Reading Consultant
Mark DeYoung
Classroom Teacher, Edina Public Schools, MN
BA in Elementary Education, Central College
MS in Curriculum & Instruction, University of MN

STONE ARCH BOOKS
MINNEAPOLIS SAN DIEGO

GN
F
NIC

Graphic Sparks are published by Stone Arch Books,
151 Good Counsel Drive, P.O. Box 669,
Mankato, Minnesota 56002.
www.stonearchbooks.com

Library of Congress Cataloging-in-Publication Data
Nickel, Scott.
　　Robot Rampage: A Buzz Beaker Brainstorm / by Scott Nickel; illustrated
by Andy J. Smith.
　　p. cm. — (Graphic Sparks. A Buzz Beaker Brainstorm)
　　ISBN-13: 978-1-59889-055-6 (hardcover)
　　ISBN-10: 1-59889-055-7 (hardcover)
　　ISBN-13: 978-1-59889-227-7 (paperback)
　　ISBN-10: 1-59889-227-4 (paperback)
　　1. Graphic novels. I. Smith, Andy J. II. Title. III. Series: Nickel, Scott. Graphic sparks.
Buzz Beaker Brainstorm.
PN6727.N544R63 2007
741.5'973—dc22　　　　　　　　　　　　　　　　　　　　　2006007699

Summary: Brainy Buzz Beaker doesn't win first prize at the school science fair. The award
goes to the weird new student, Elron, instead. Then Elron's homemade robot goes haywire,
and Buzz gets taken on a wild, rampaging ride!

Art Director: Heather Kindseth
Graphic Designer: Brann Garvey

1 2 3 4 5 6 11 10 09 08 07 06

Printed in the United States of America

ROBOT RAMPAGE

A BUZZ BEAKER BRAINSTORM

by Scott Nickel

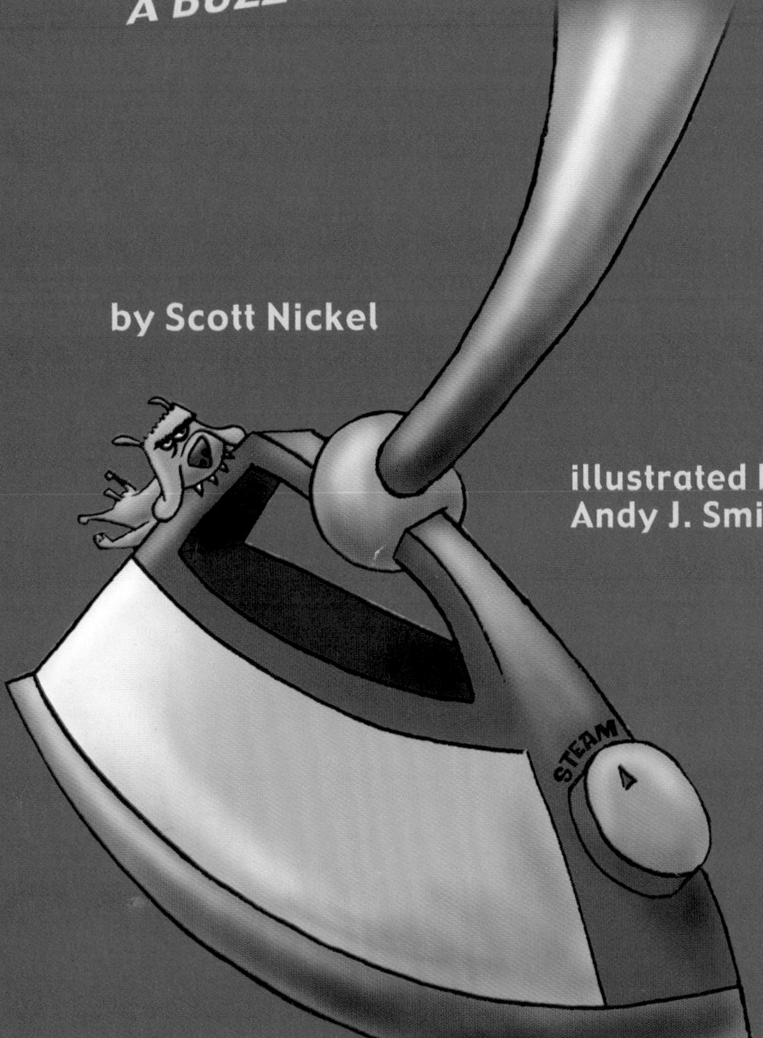
STEAM

illustrated by
Andy J. Smith

ROBOT RAMPAGE

CAST OF CHARACTERS

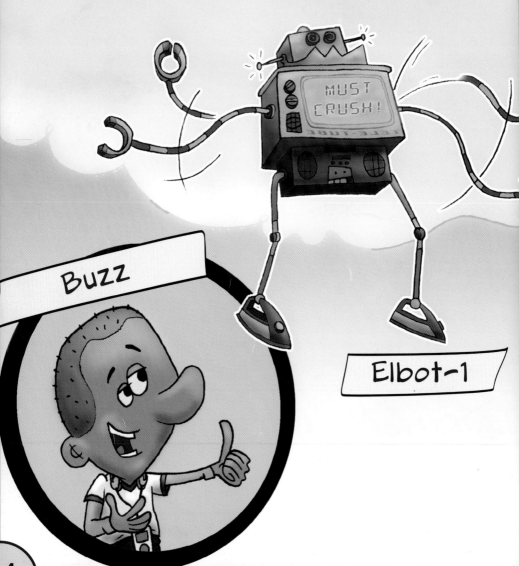

MUST CRUSH!

Buzz

Elbot-1

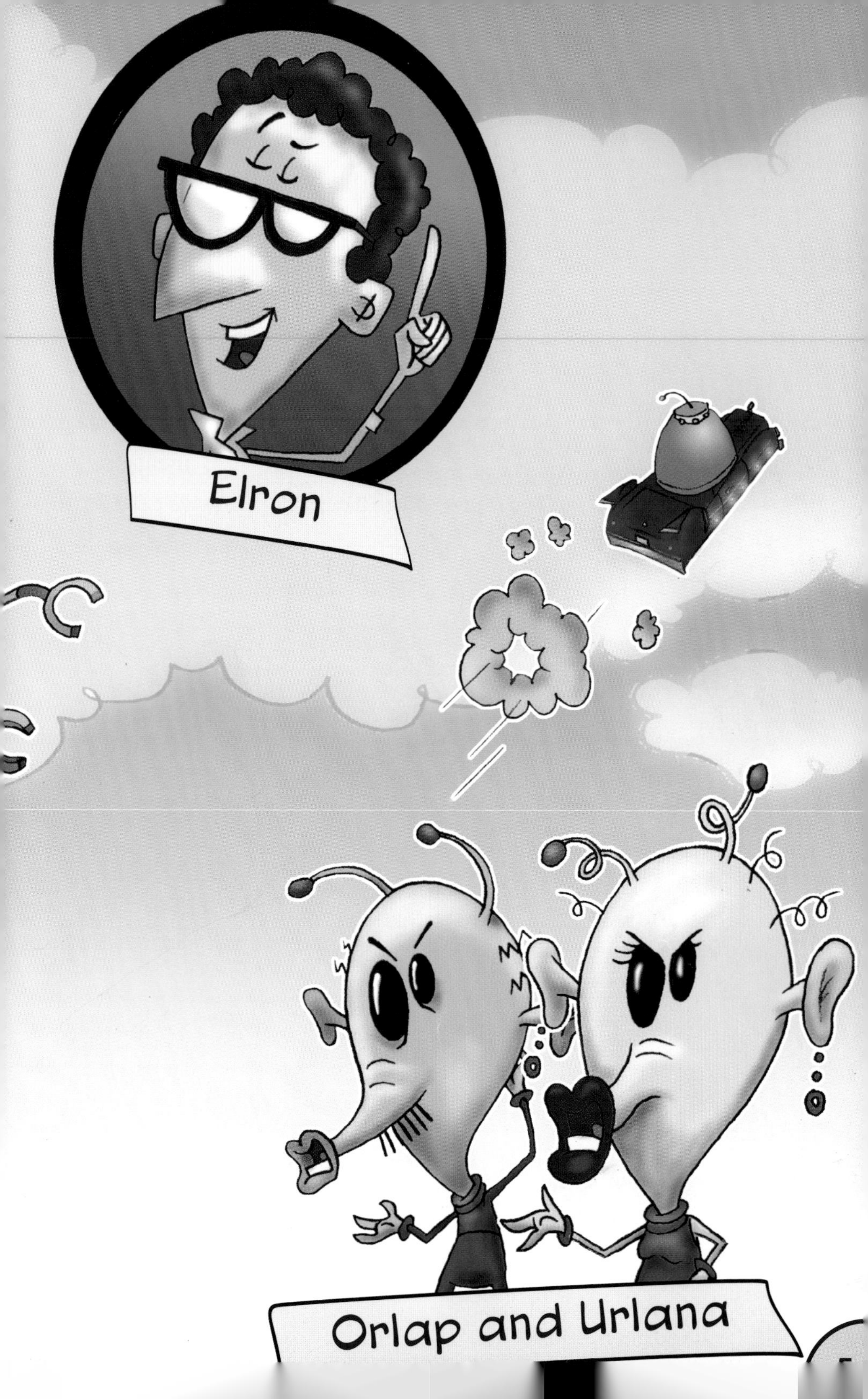
Elron
Orlap and Urlana

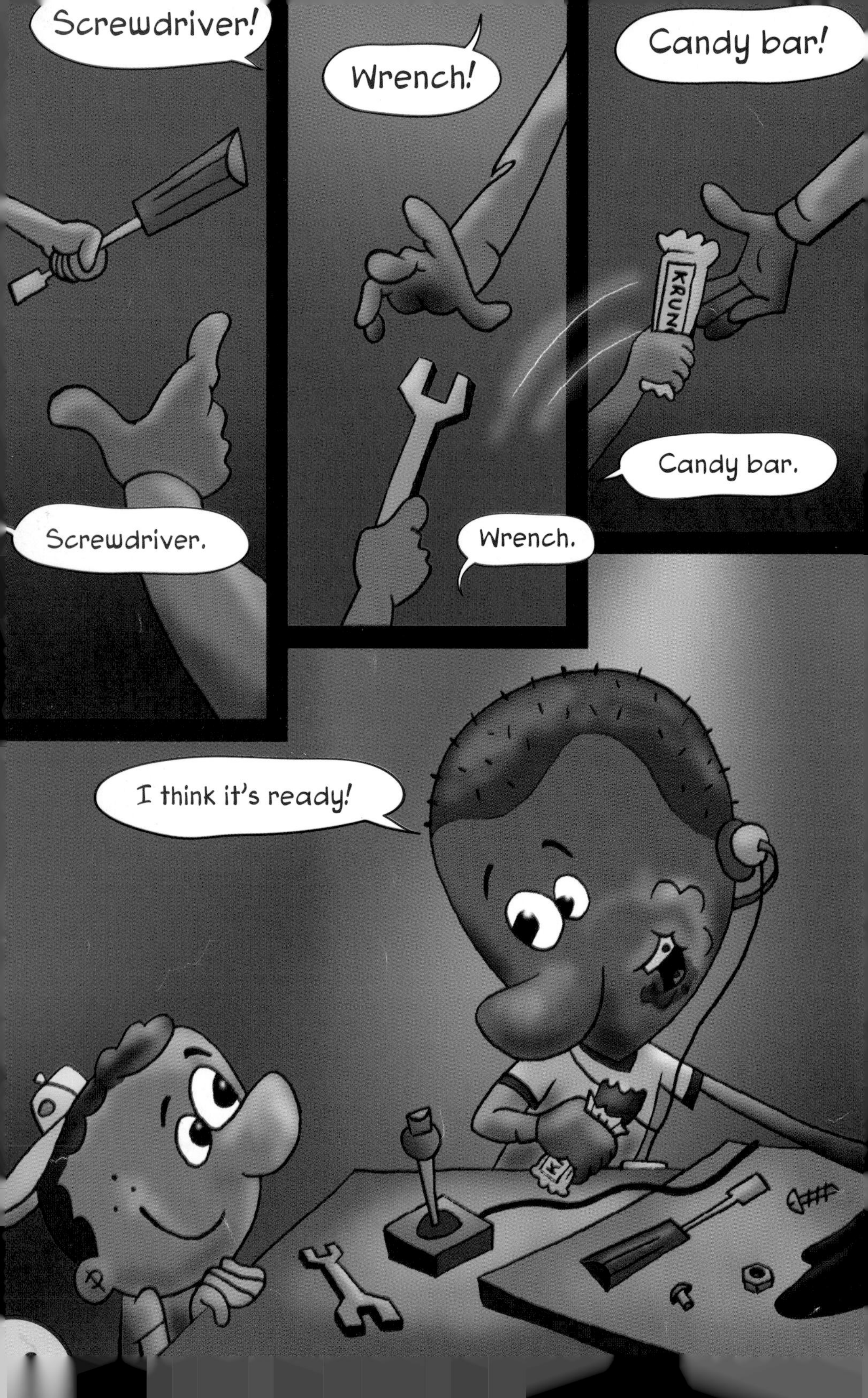
Screwdriver!
Screwdriver.
Wrench!
Wrench.
Candy bar!
KRUNG
Candy bar.
I think it's ready!

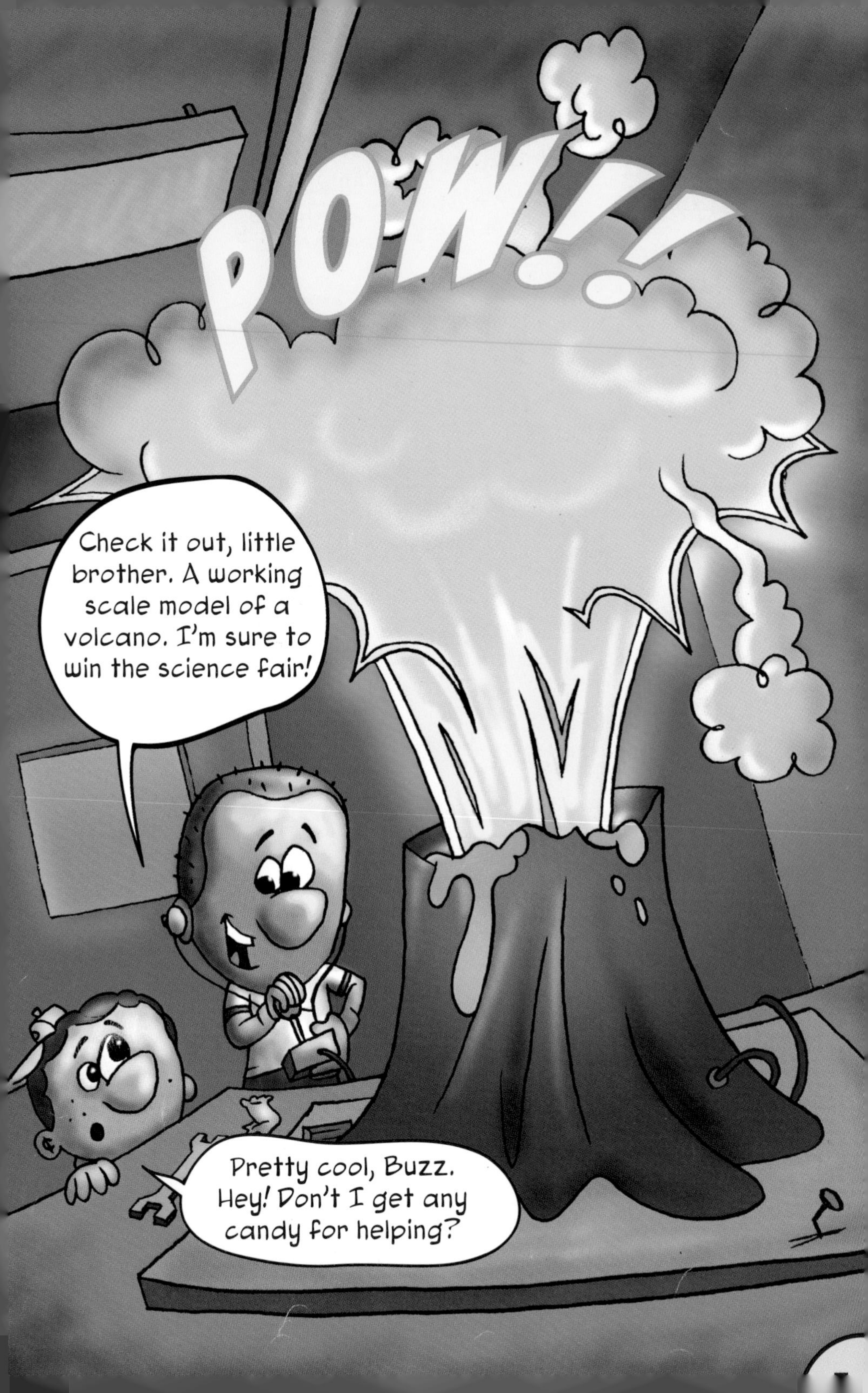
POW!!
Check it out, little brother. A working scale model of a volcano. I'm sure to win the science fair!
Pretty cool, Buzz. Hey! Don't I get any candy for helping?

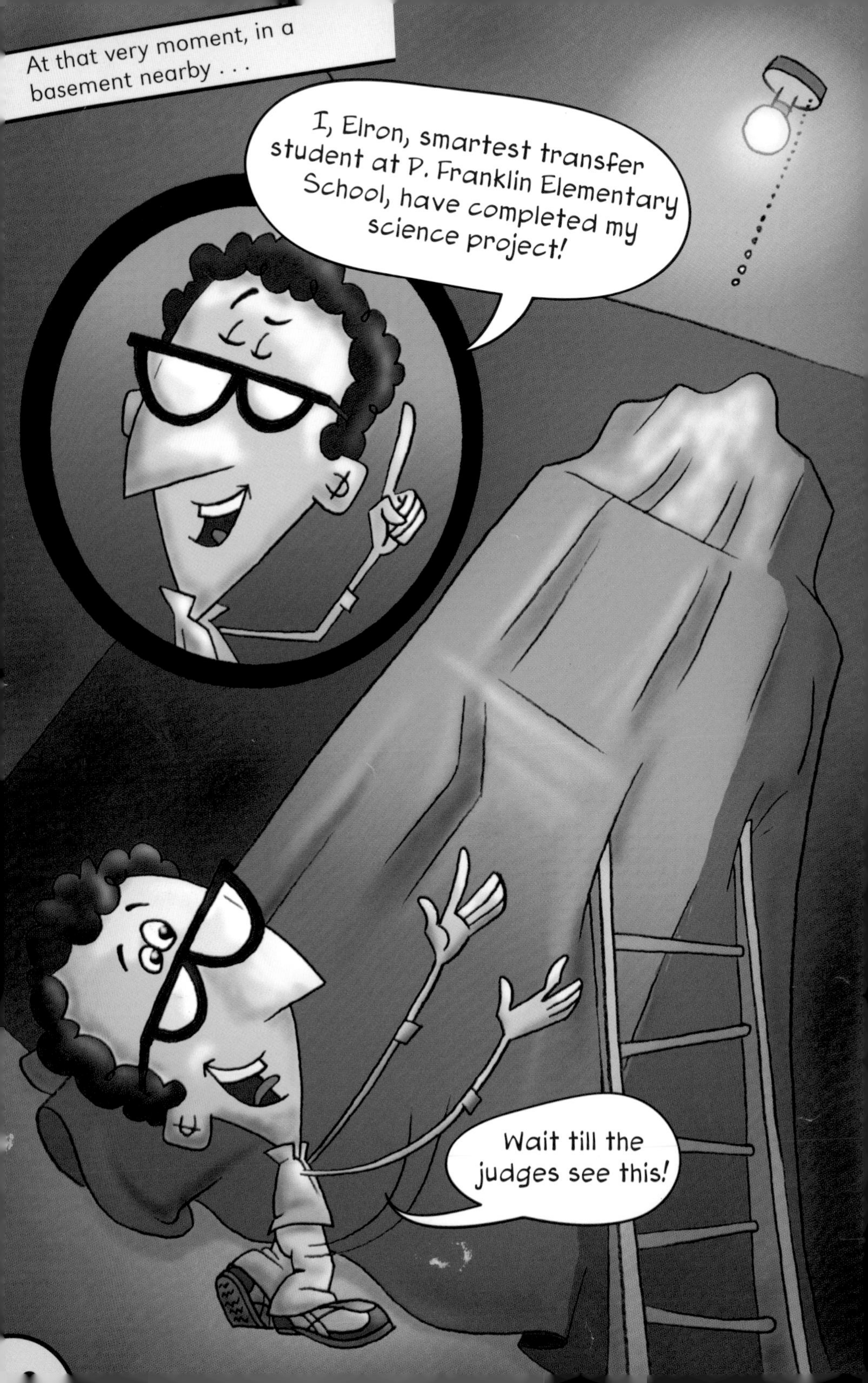
At that very moment, in a basement nearby . . .
I, Elron, smartest transfer student at P. Franklin Elementary School, have completed my science project!
Wait till the judges see this!

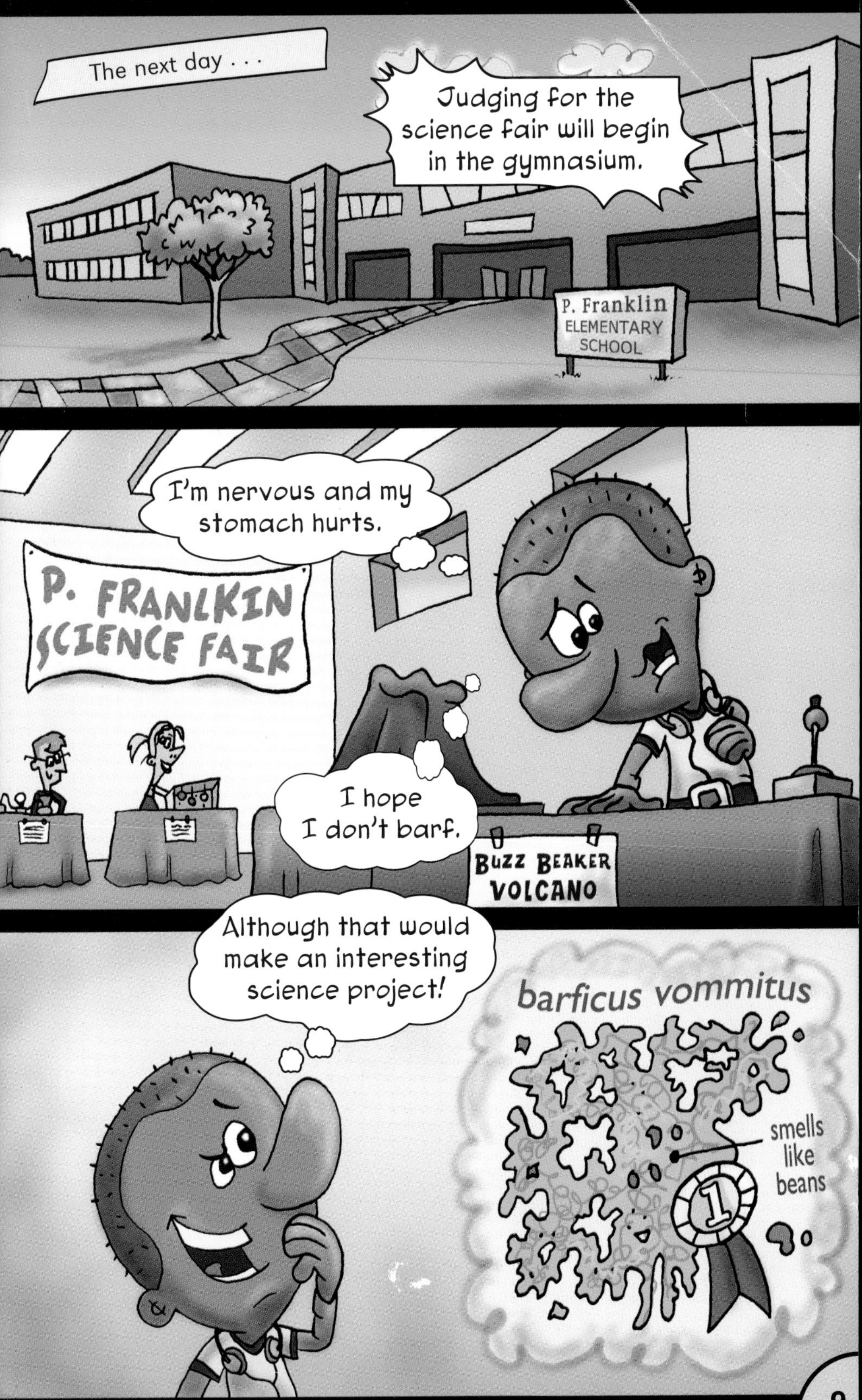
The next day . . .
Judging for the science fair will begin in the gymnasium.
P. Franklin ELEMENTARY SCHOOL
I'm nervous and my stomach hurts.
P. FRANKLIN SCIENCE FAIR
I hope I don't barf.
BUZZ BEAKER VOLCANO
Although that would make an interesting science project!
barficus vommitus
smells like beans
1

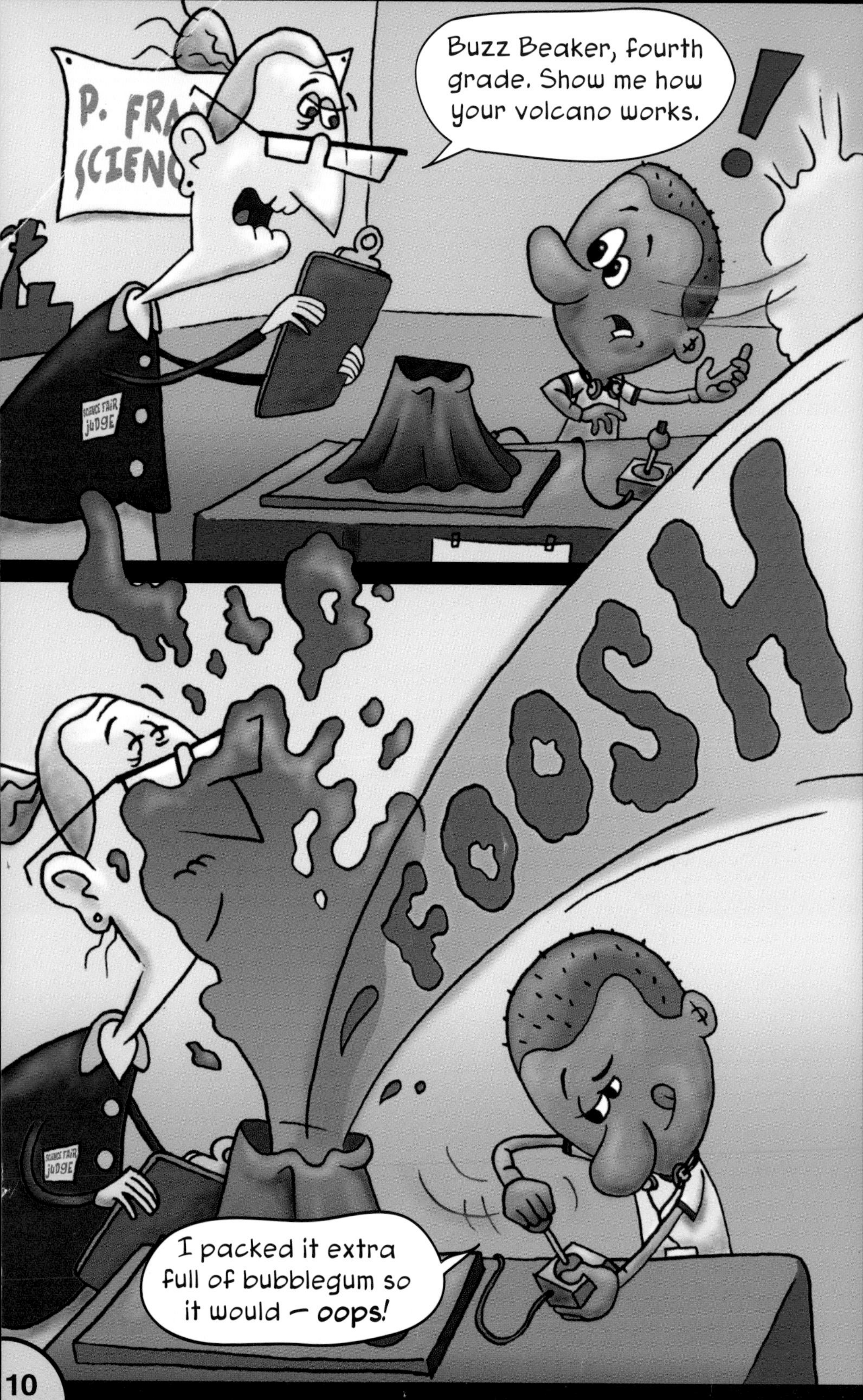
P. FRA
SCIENC
Buzz Beaker, fourth grade. Show me how your volcano works.
SCIENCE FAIR JUDGE
FOOSH
SCIENCE FAIR JUDGE
I packed it extra full of bubblegum so it would — *oops!*

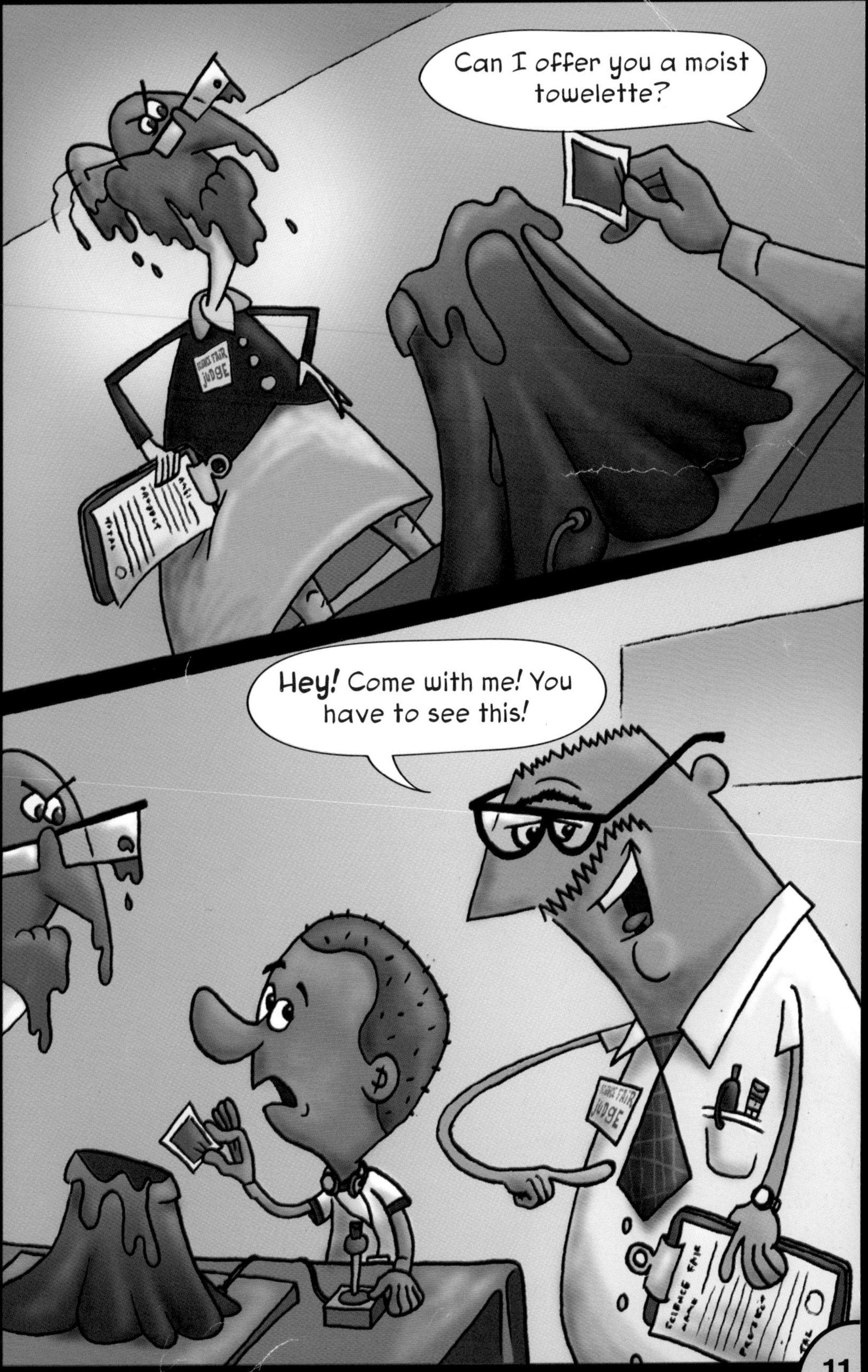

Can I offer you a moist towelette?
Hey! Come with me! You have to see this!
SCIENCE FAIR JUDGE

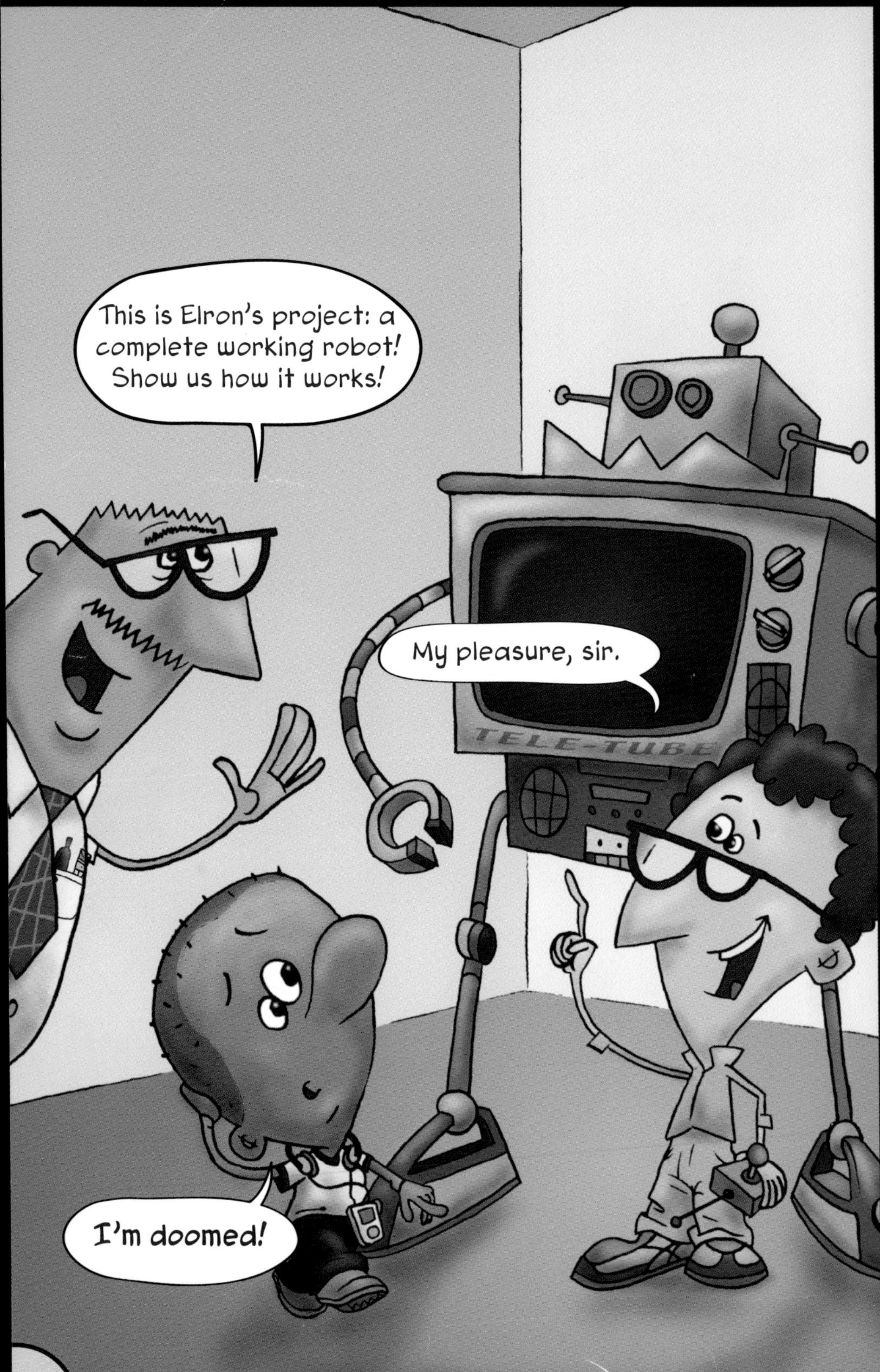
This is Elron's project: a complete working robot! Show us how it works!
My pleasure, sir.
TELE-TUBE
I'm doomed!

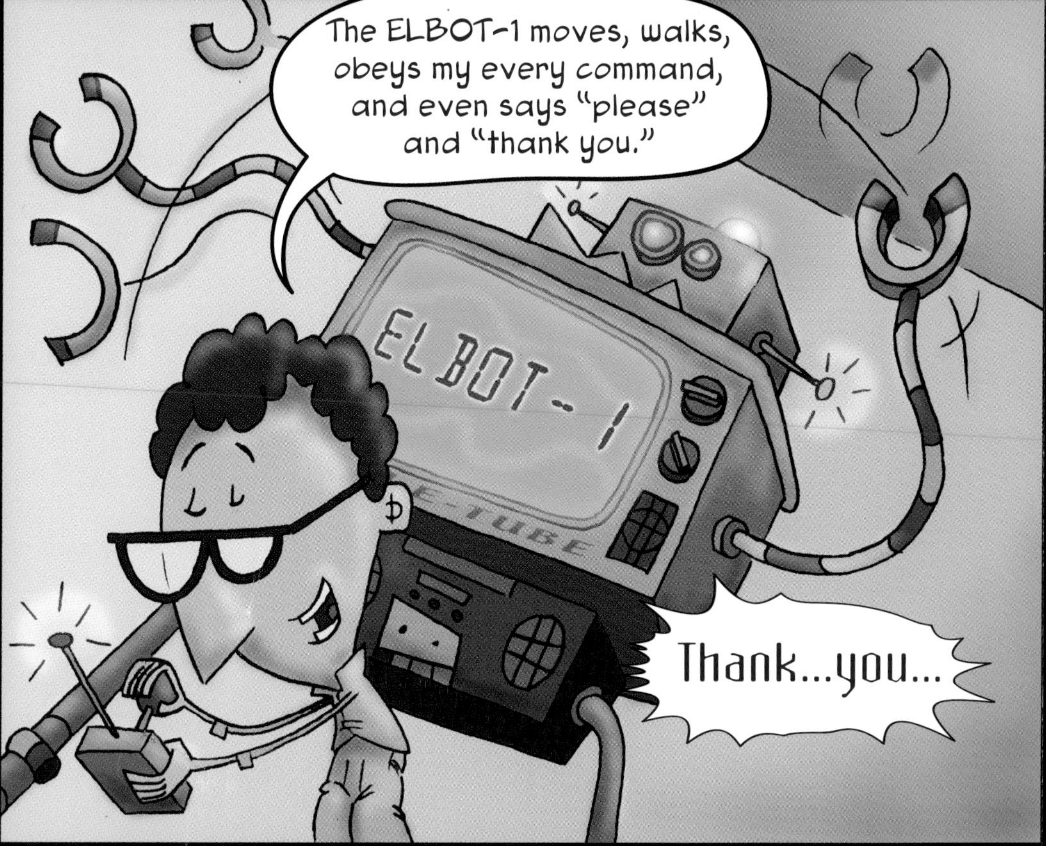
The ELBOT-1 moves, walks, obeys my every command, and even says "please" and "thank you."
EL BOT - 1
Thank...you...

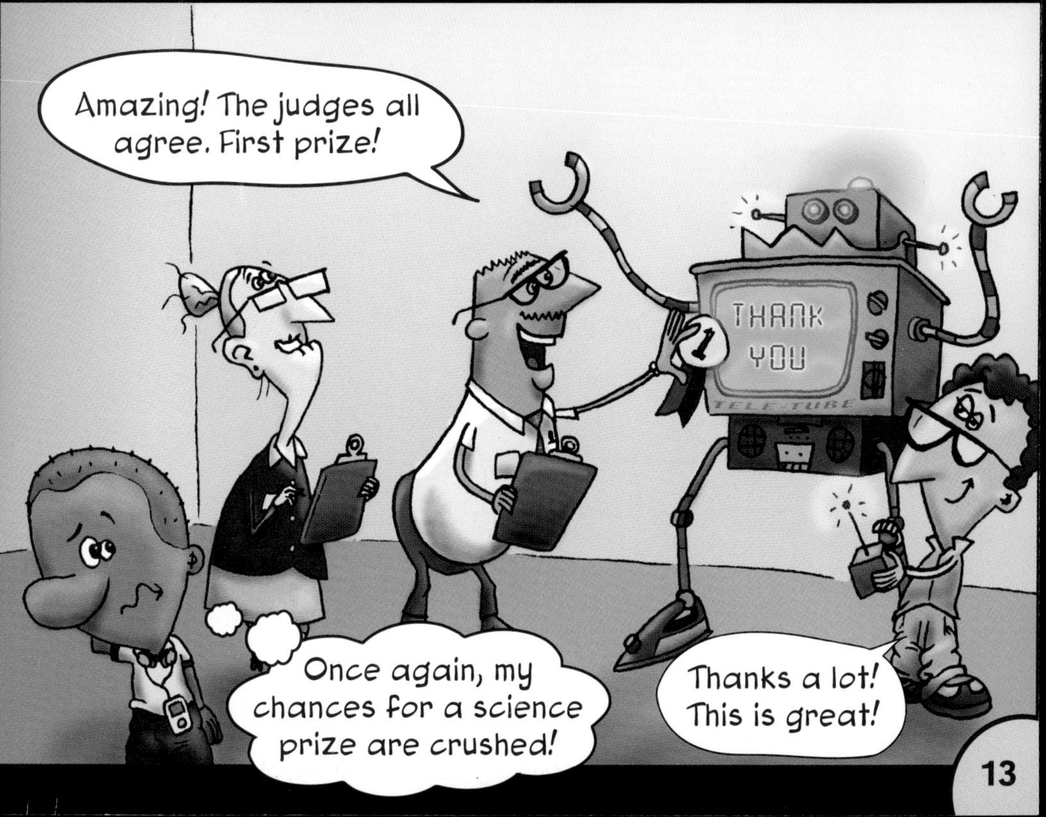
Amazing! The judges all agree. First prize!
THANK YOU
Once again, my chances for a science prize are crushed!
Thanks a lot! This is great!

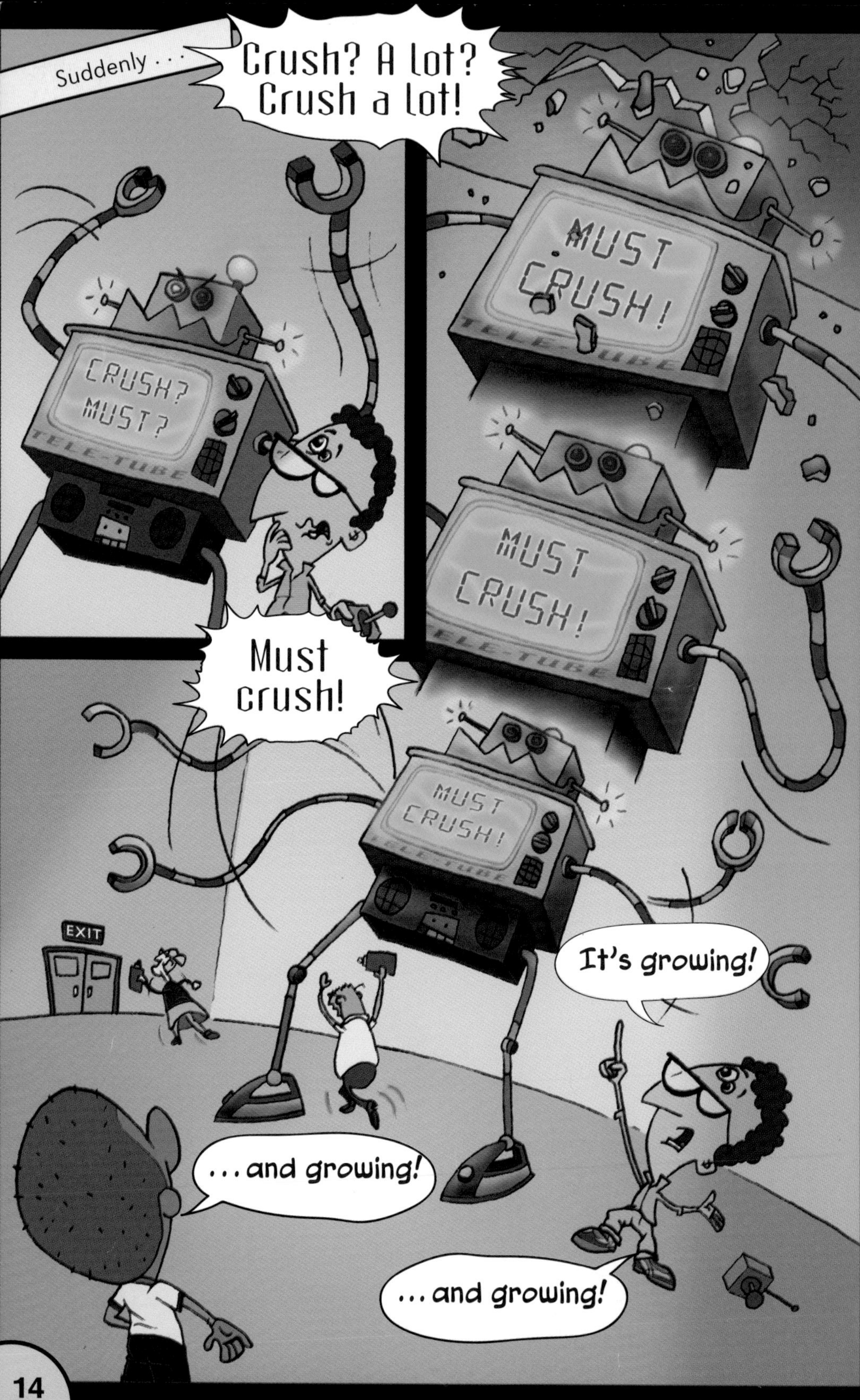
Suddenly . . .
Crush? A lot? Crush a lot!
CRUSH? MUST?
TELE-TUBE
MUST CRUSH!
MUST CRUSH!
Must crush!
MUST CRUSH!
EXIT
It's growing!
. . . and growing!
. . . and growing!

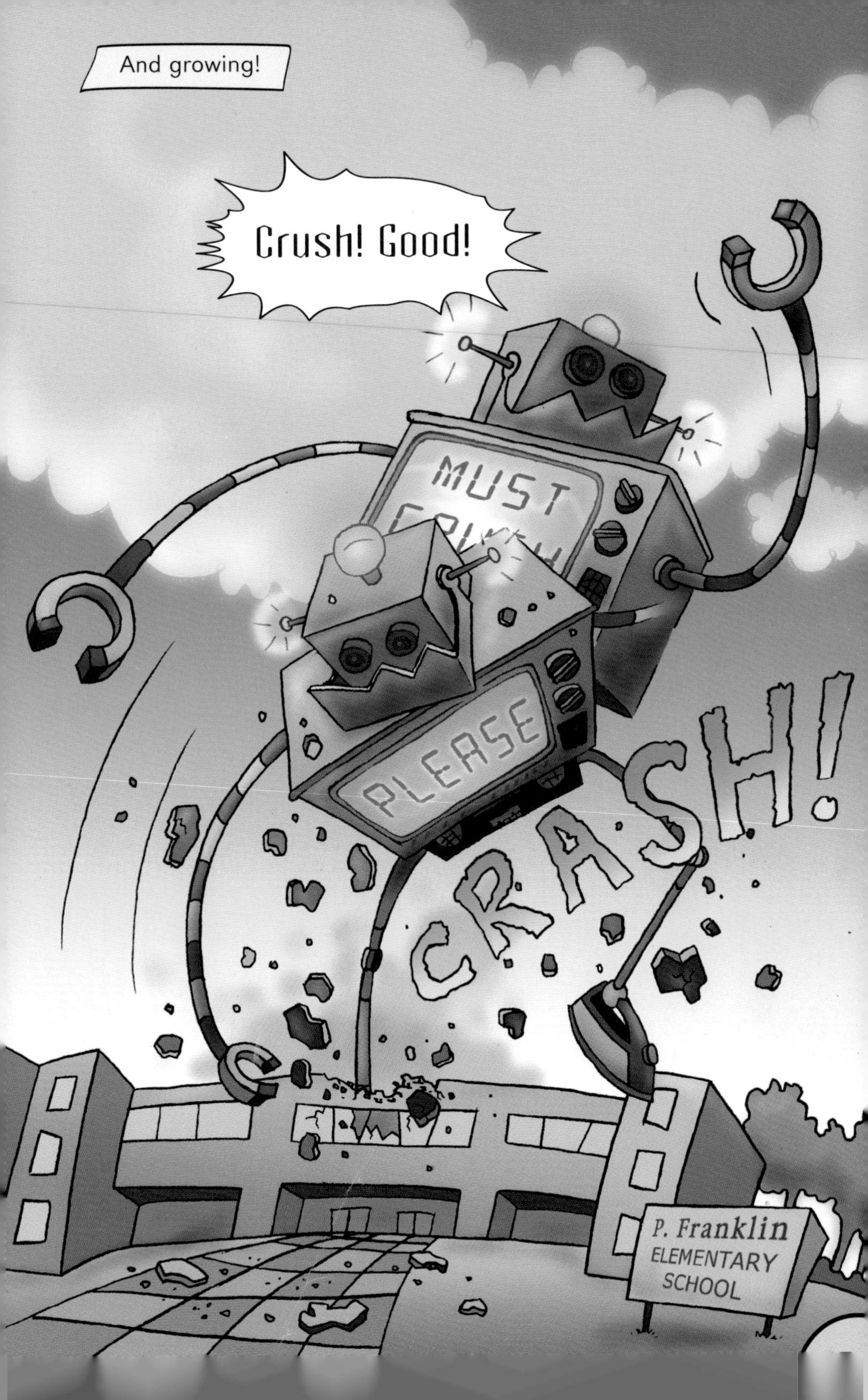
And growing!
Crush! Good!
MUST
PLEASE
CRASH!
P. Franklin
ELEMENTARY
SCHOOL

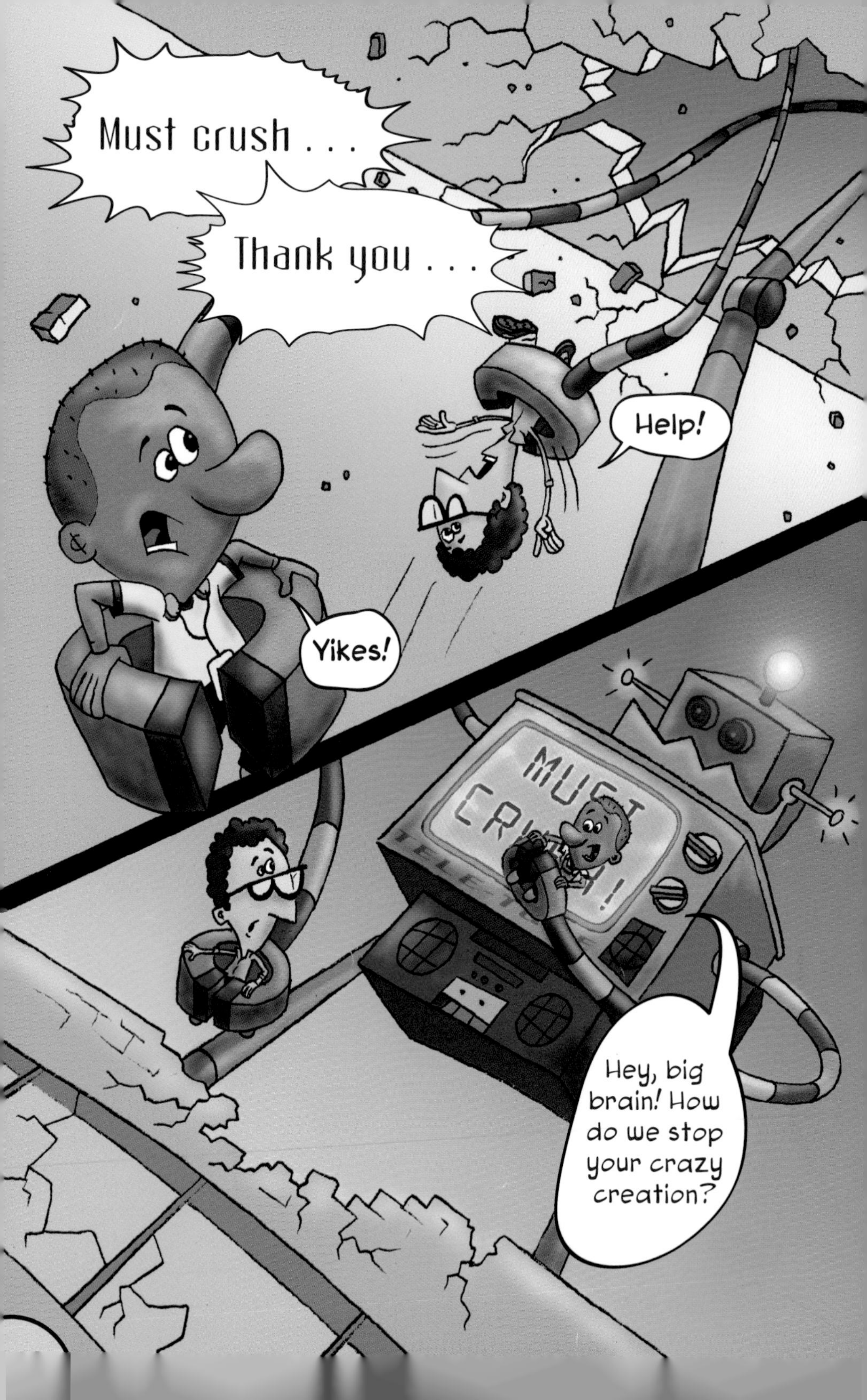
Must crush . . .
Thank you . . .
Help!
Yikes!
MUST CRUSH!
Hey, big brain! How do we stop your crazy creation?

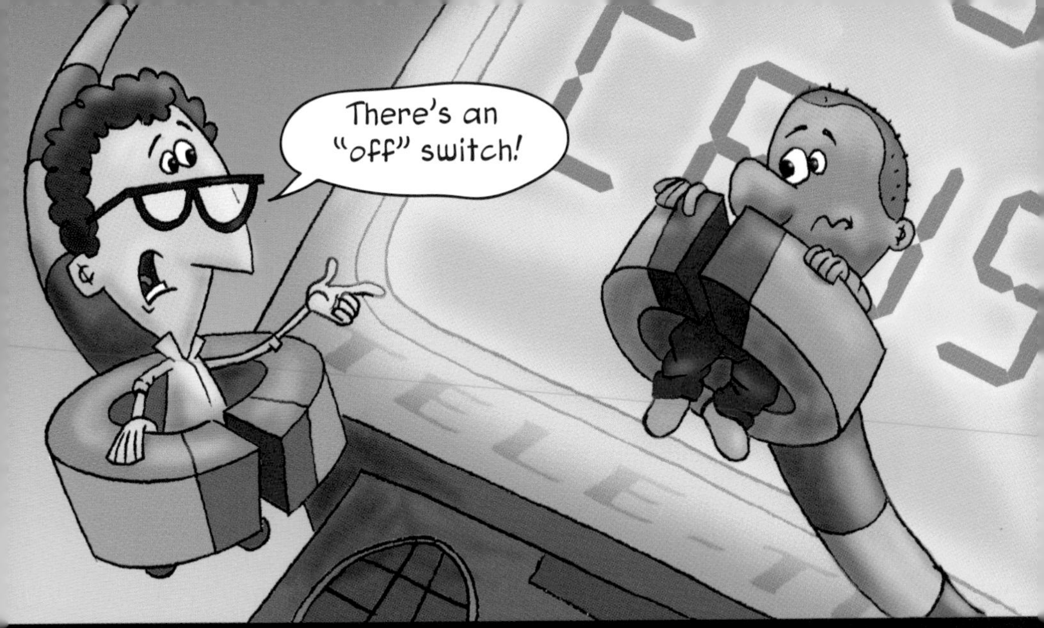
There's an "off" switch!

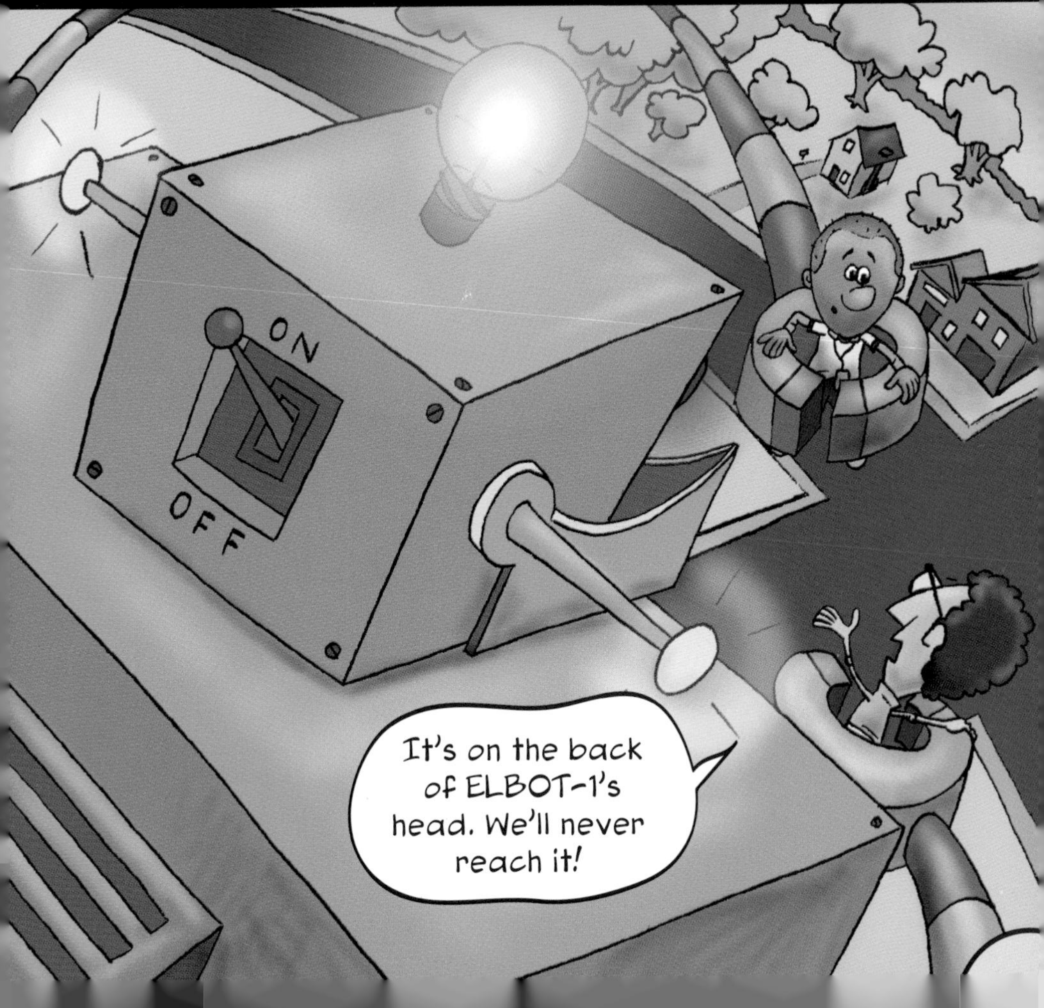
ON
OFF
It's on the back of ELBOT-1's head. We'll never reach it!

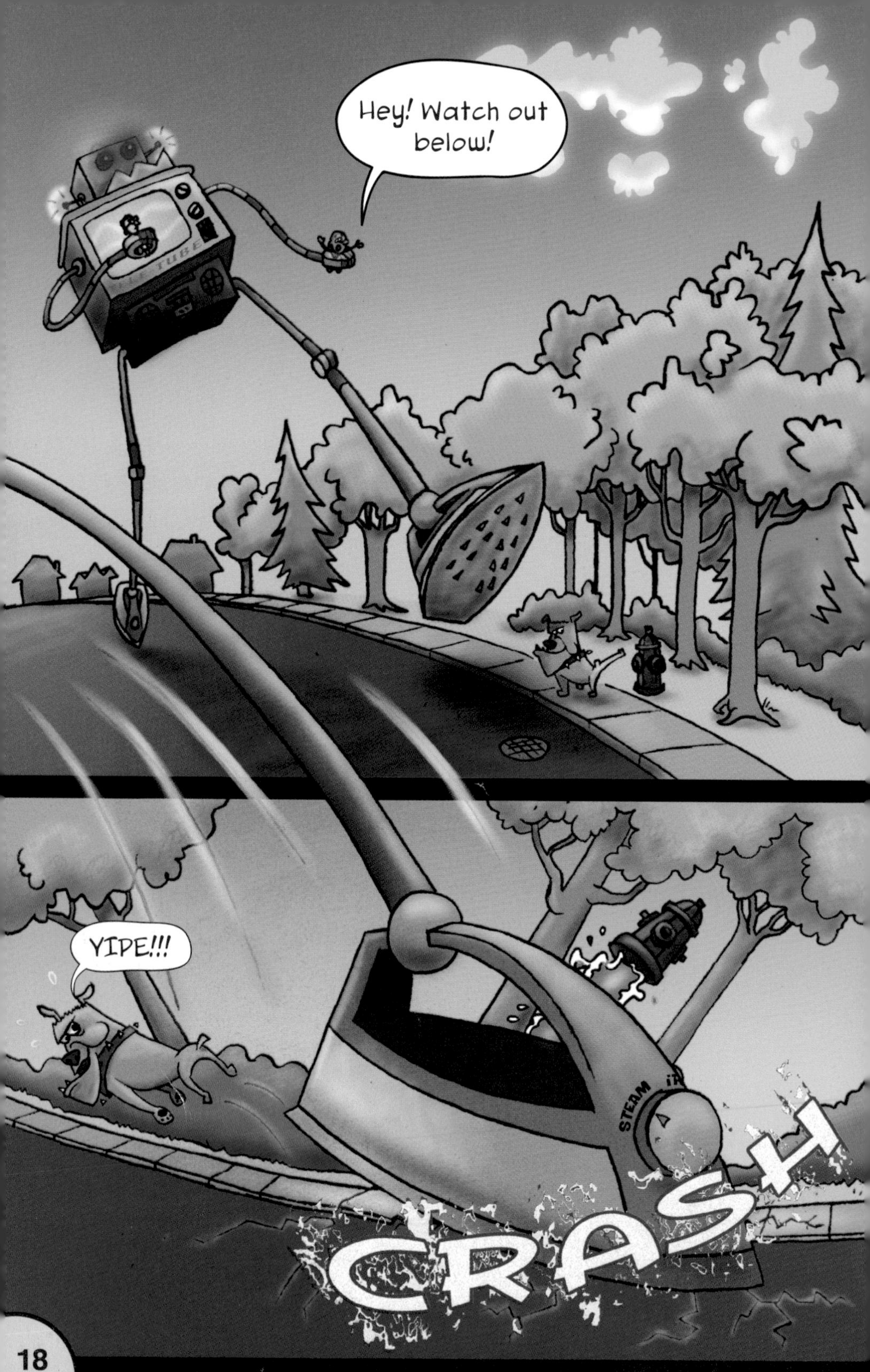
Hey! Watch out below!
YIPE!!!
STEAM
CRASH

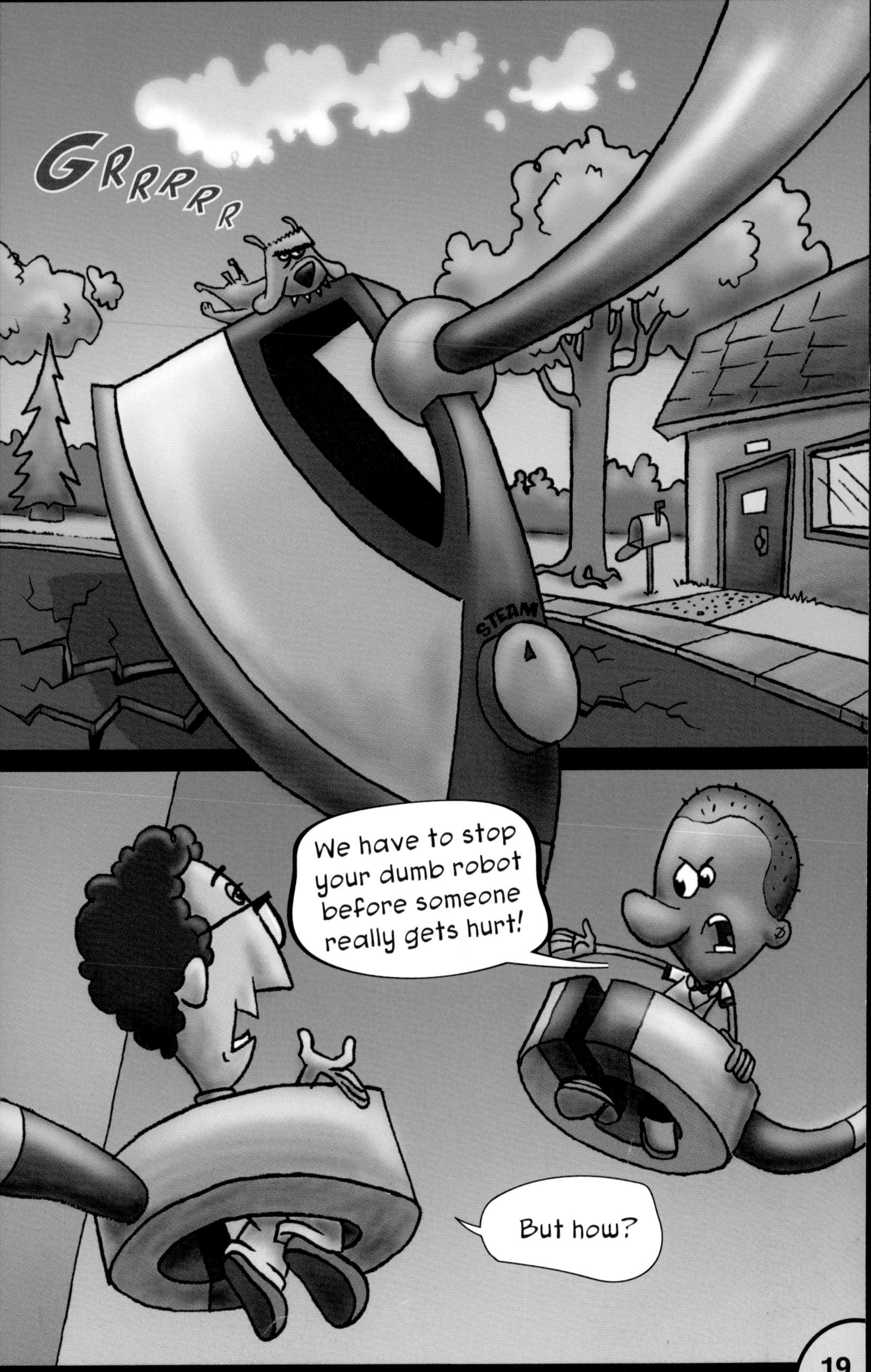
GRRRRR
STEAM
We have to stop your dumb robot before someone really gets hurt!
But how?

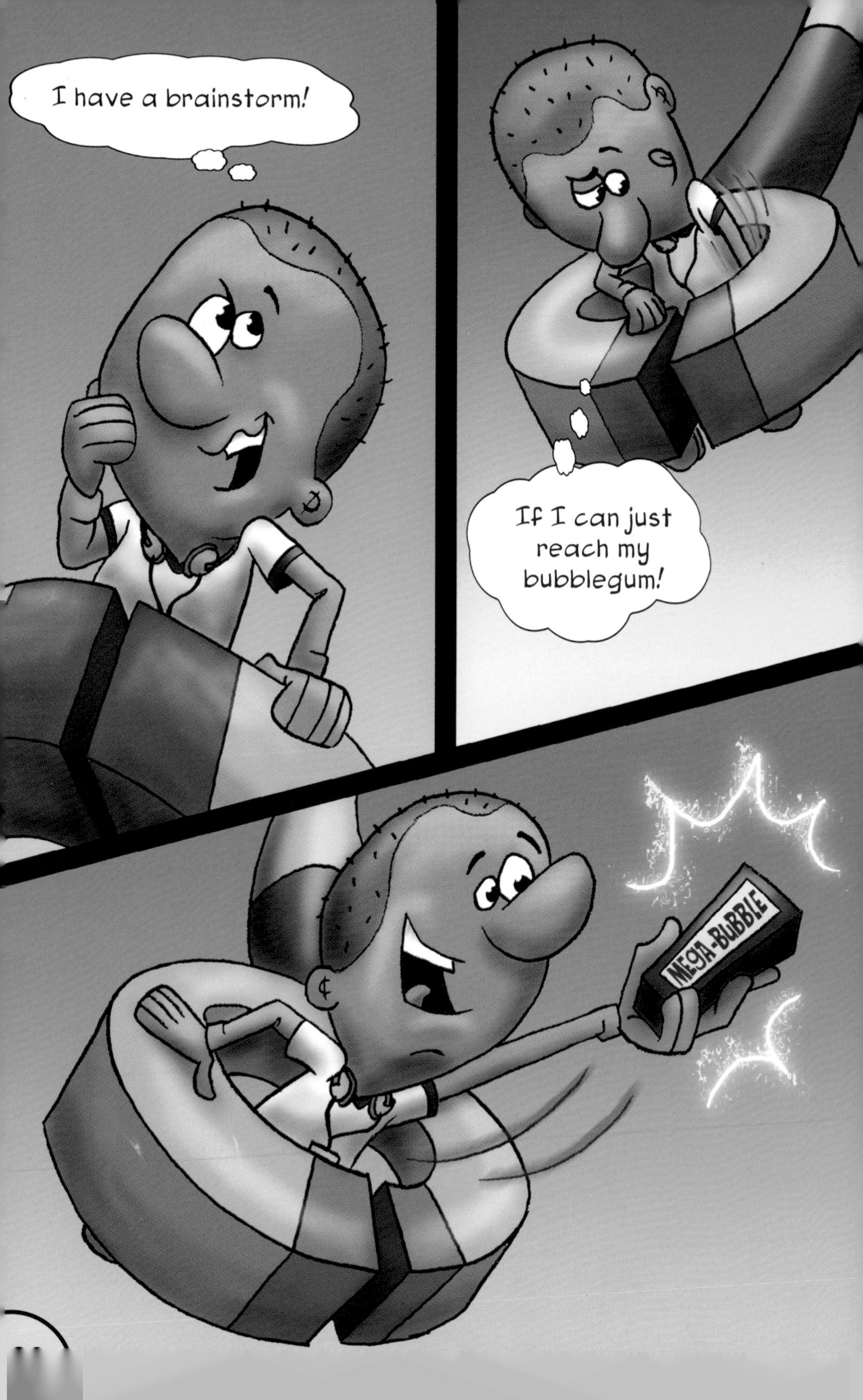
I have a brainstorm!
If I can just reach my bubblegum!
MEGA-BUBBLE

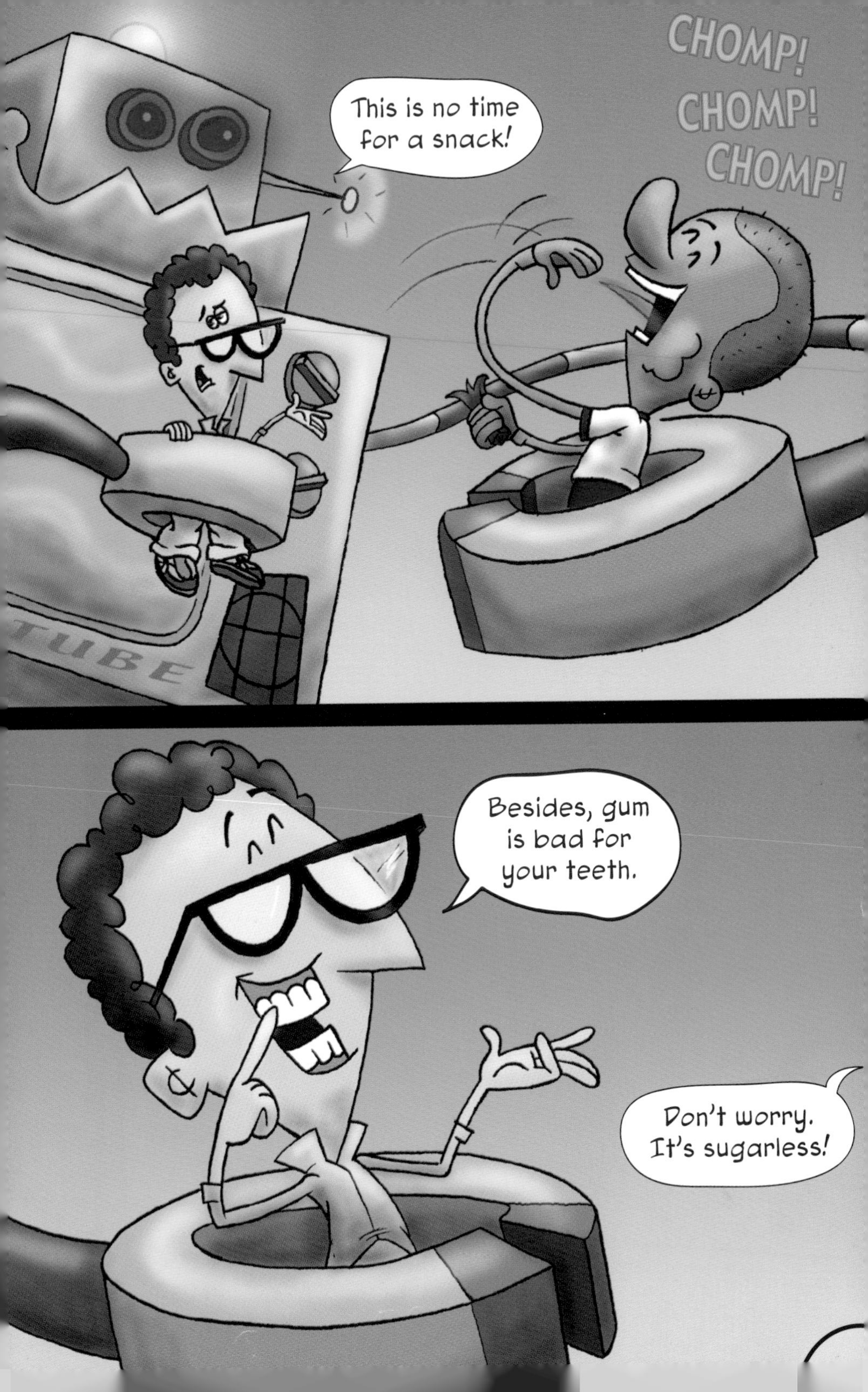
This is no time for a snack!
CHOMP! CHOMP! CHOMP!
TUBE
Besides, gum is bad for your teeth.
Don't worry. It's sugarless!

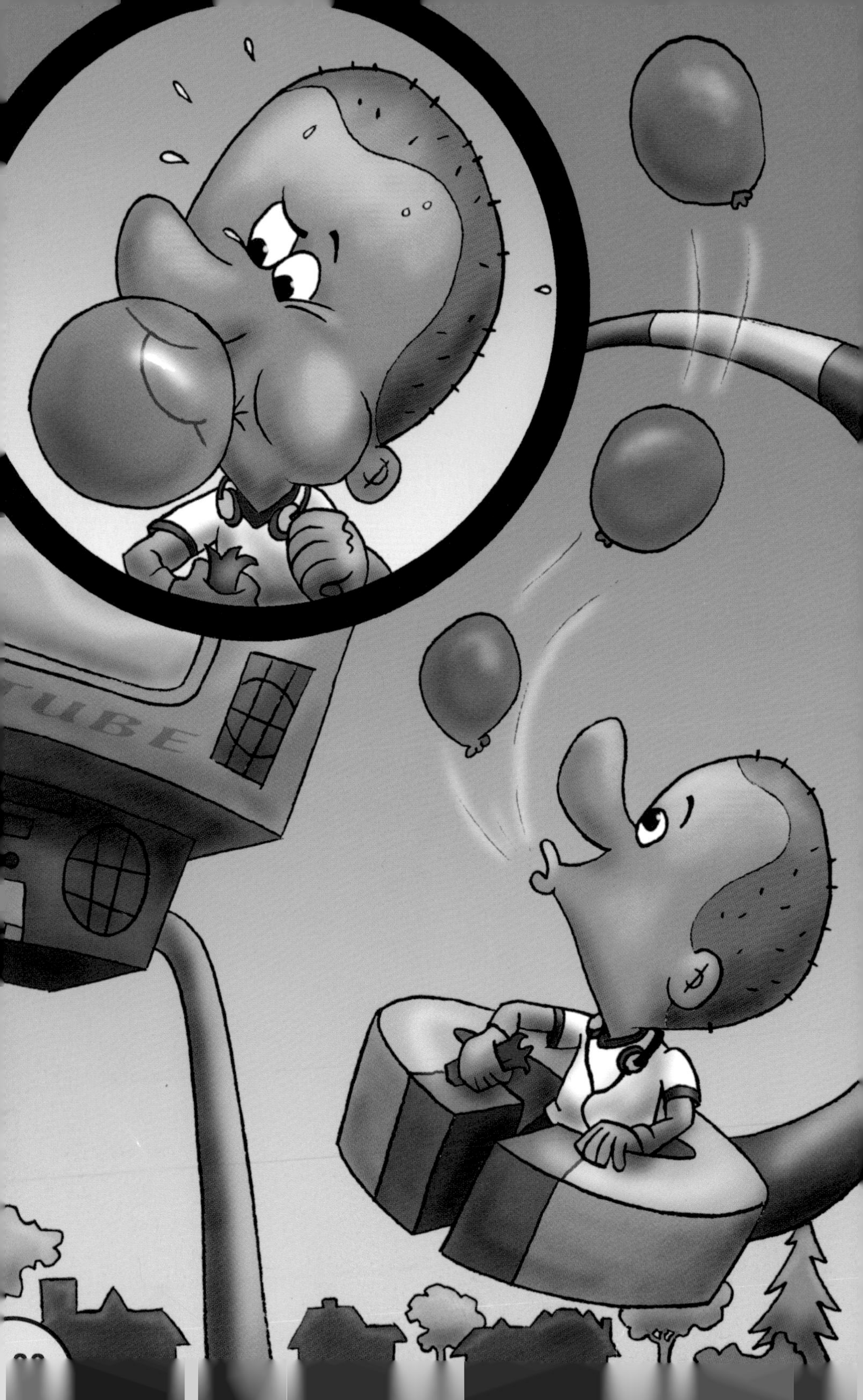
TUBE

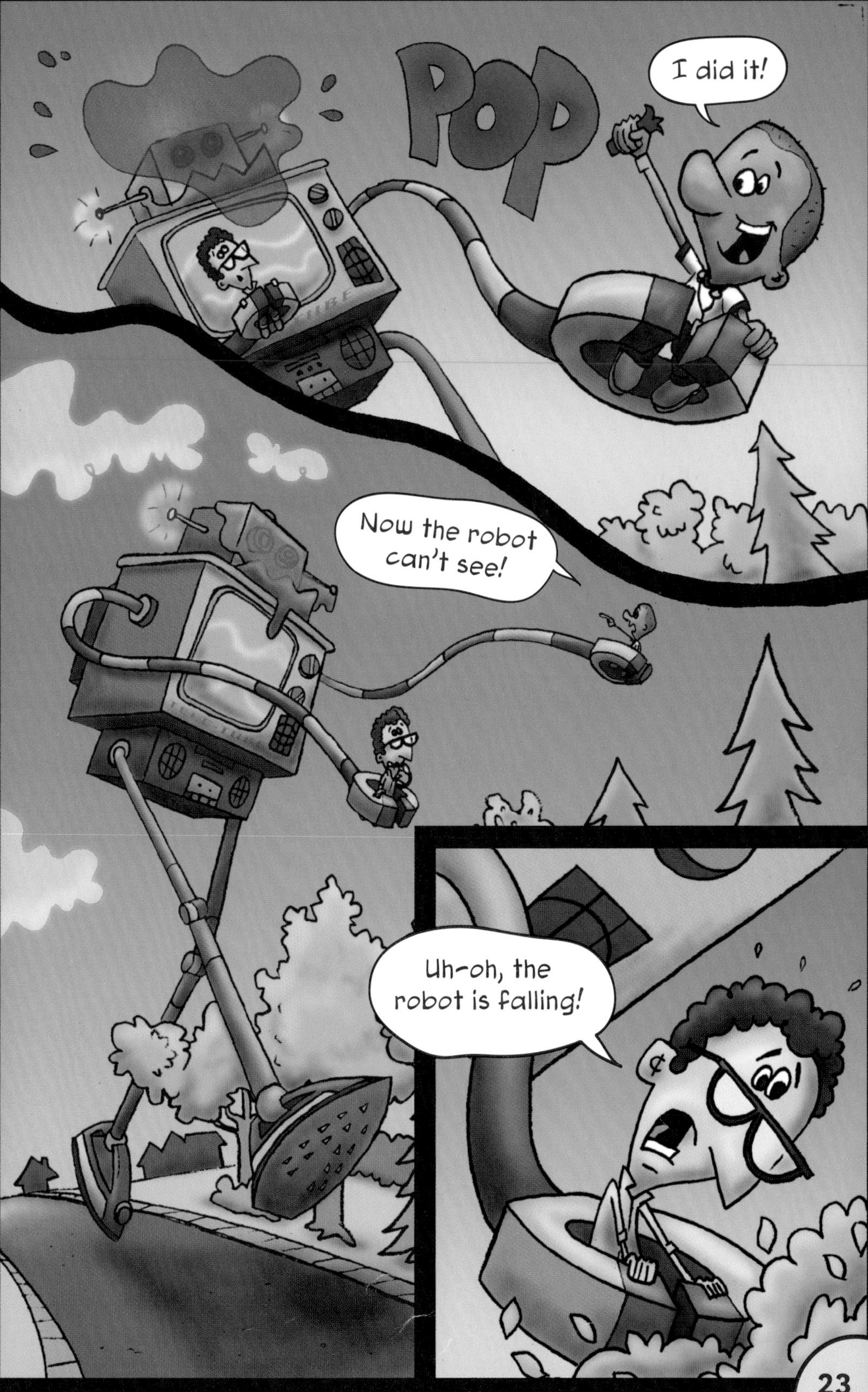
POP
I did it!
Now the robot can't see!
Uh-oh, the robot is falling!

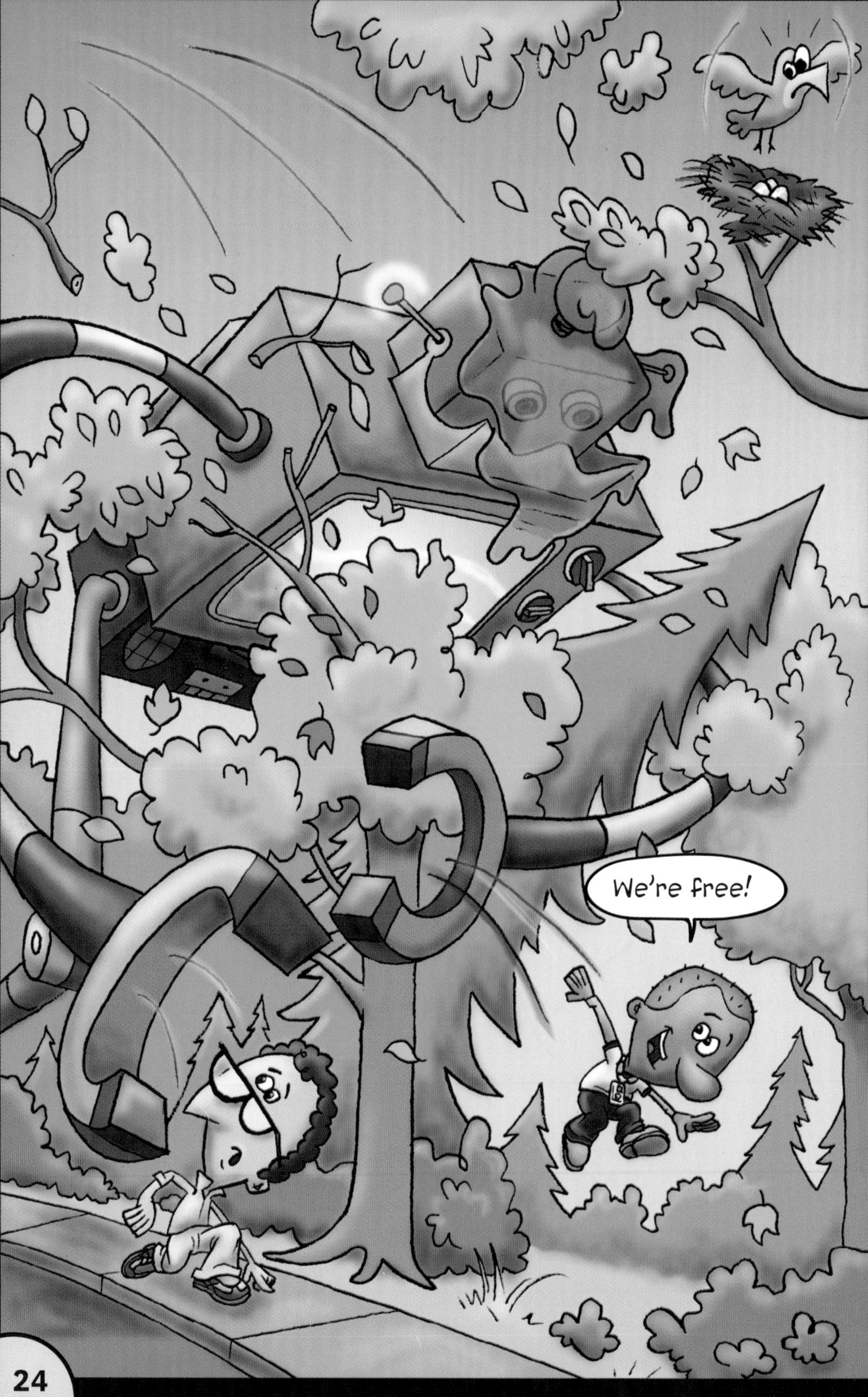
We're free!

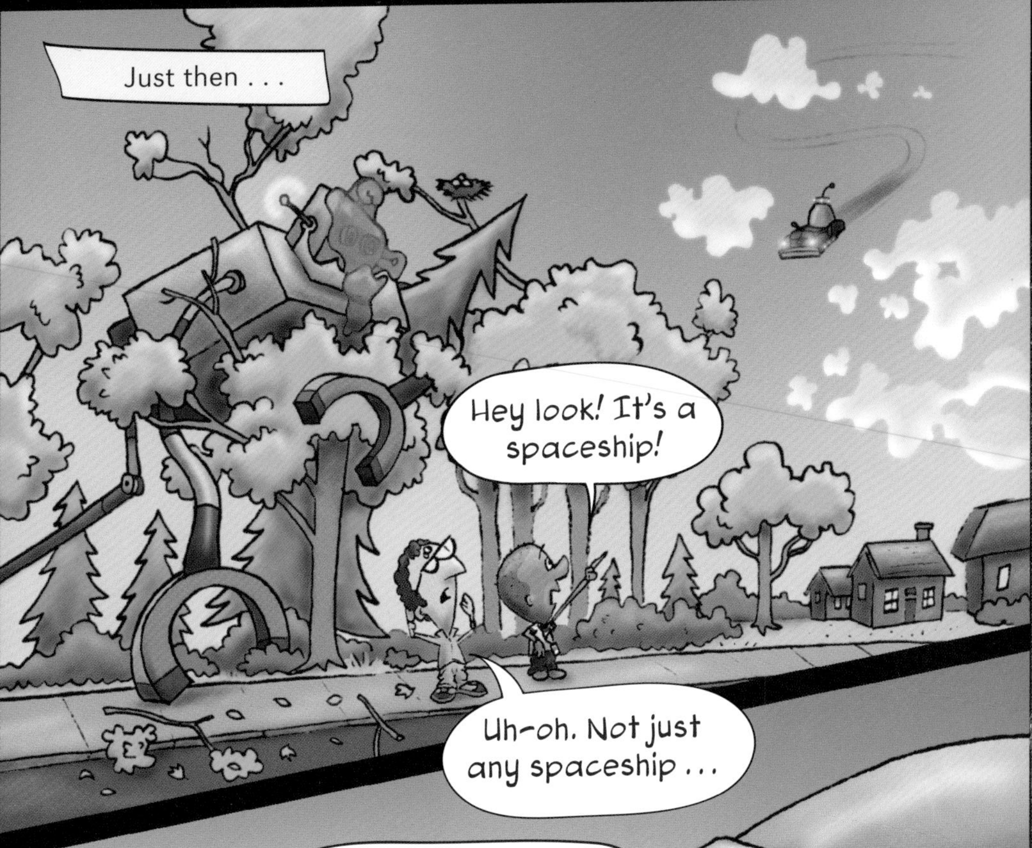
Just then . . .
Hey look! It's a spaceship!
Uh-oh. Not just any spaceship . . .

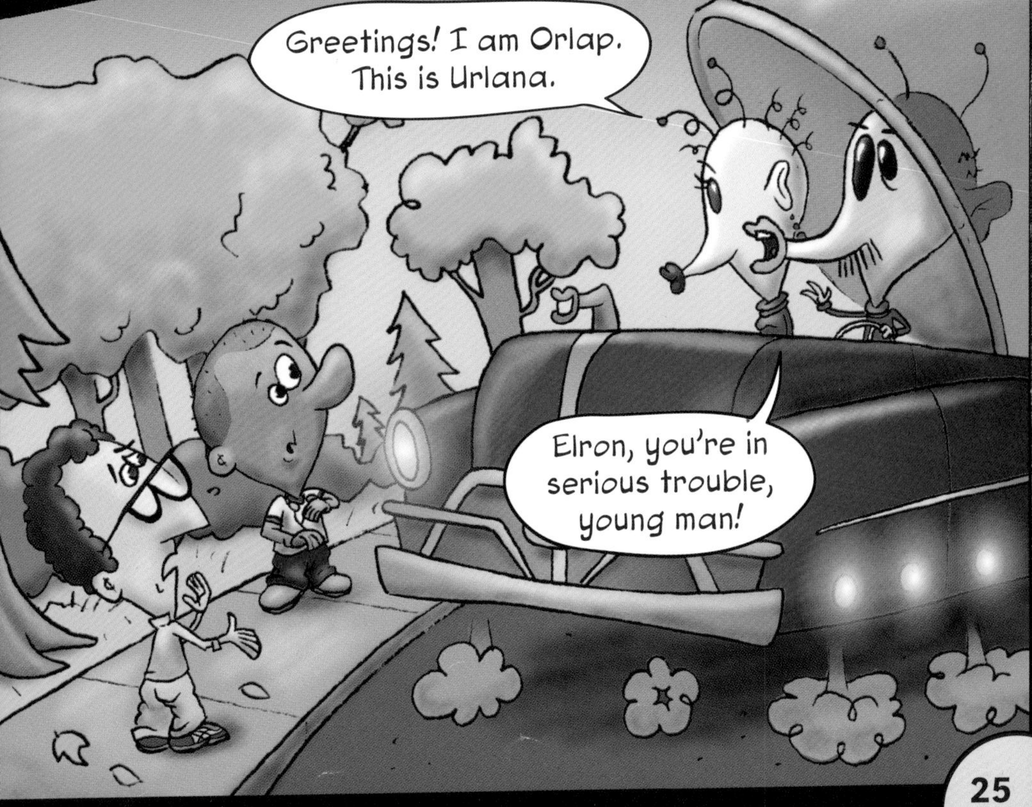
Greetings! I am Orlap. This is Urlana.
Elron, you're in serious trouble, young man!

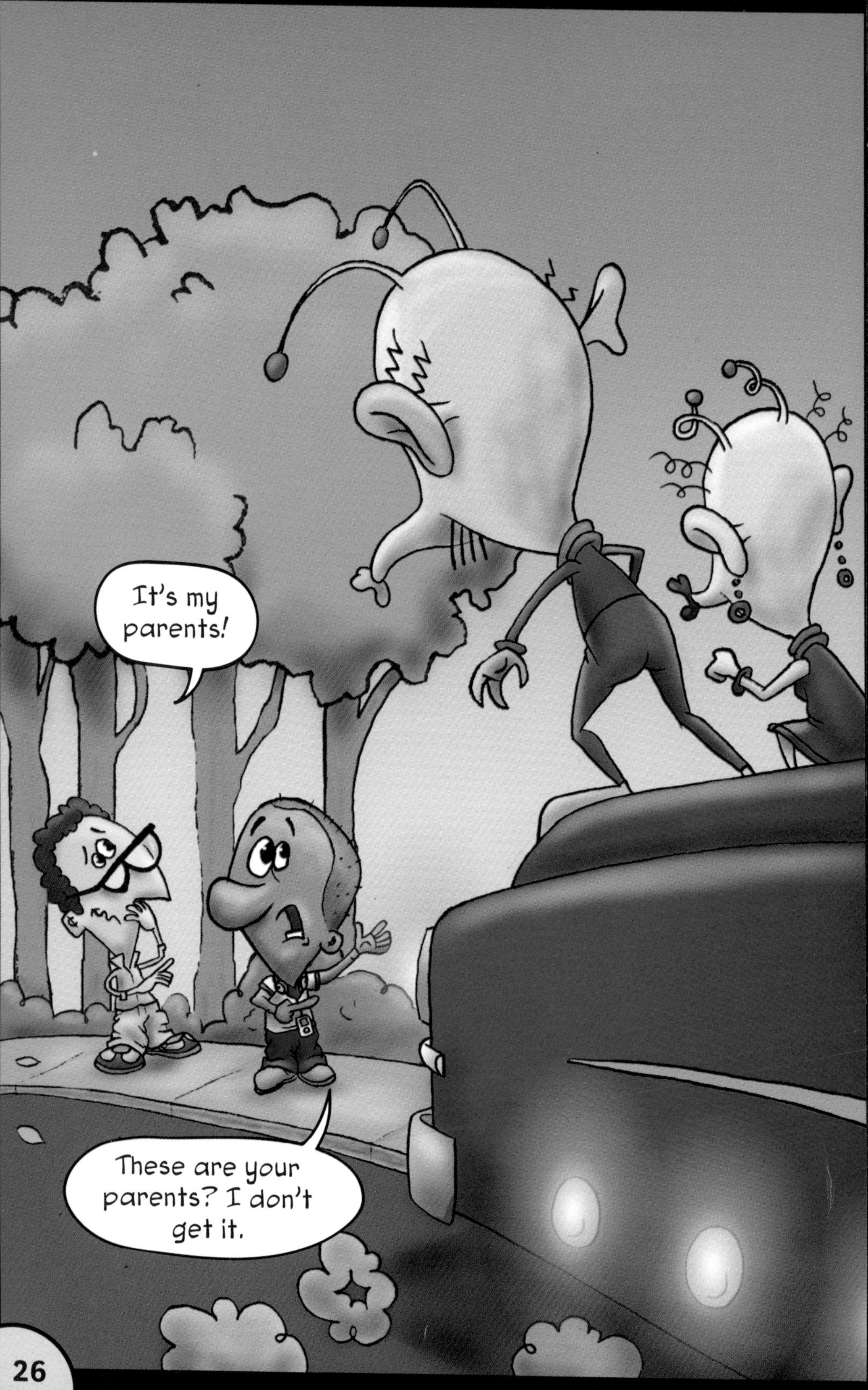
It's my parents!
These are your parents? I don't get it.

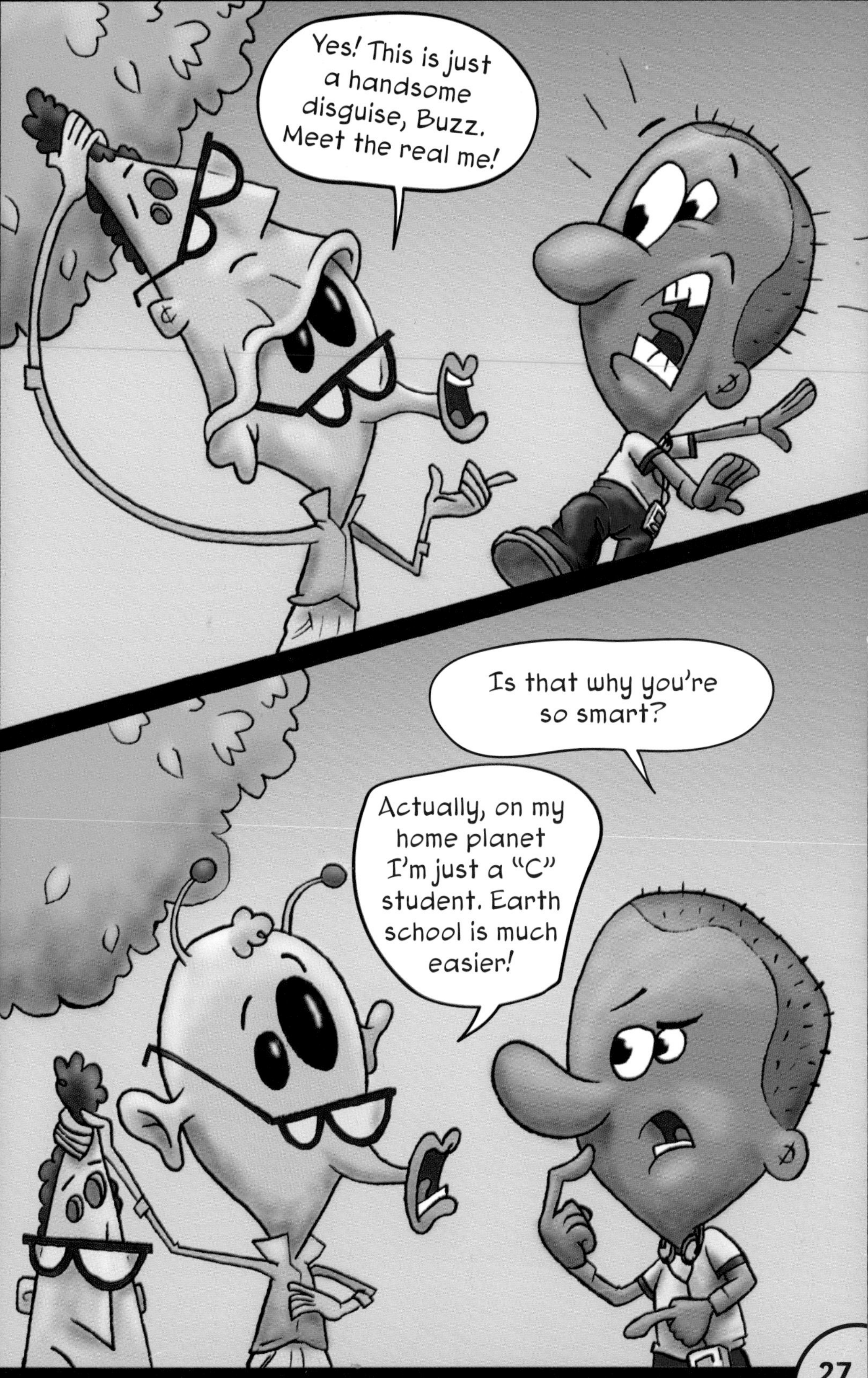
Yes! This is just a handsome disguise, Buzz. Meet the real me!
Is that why you're so smart?
Actually, on my home planet I'm just a "C" student. Earth school is much easier!

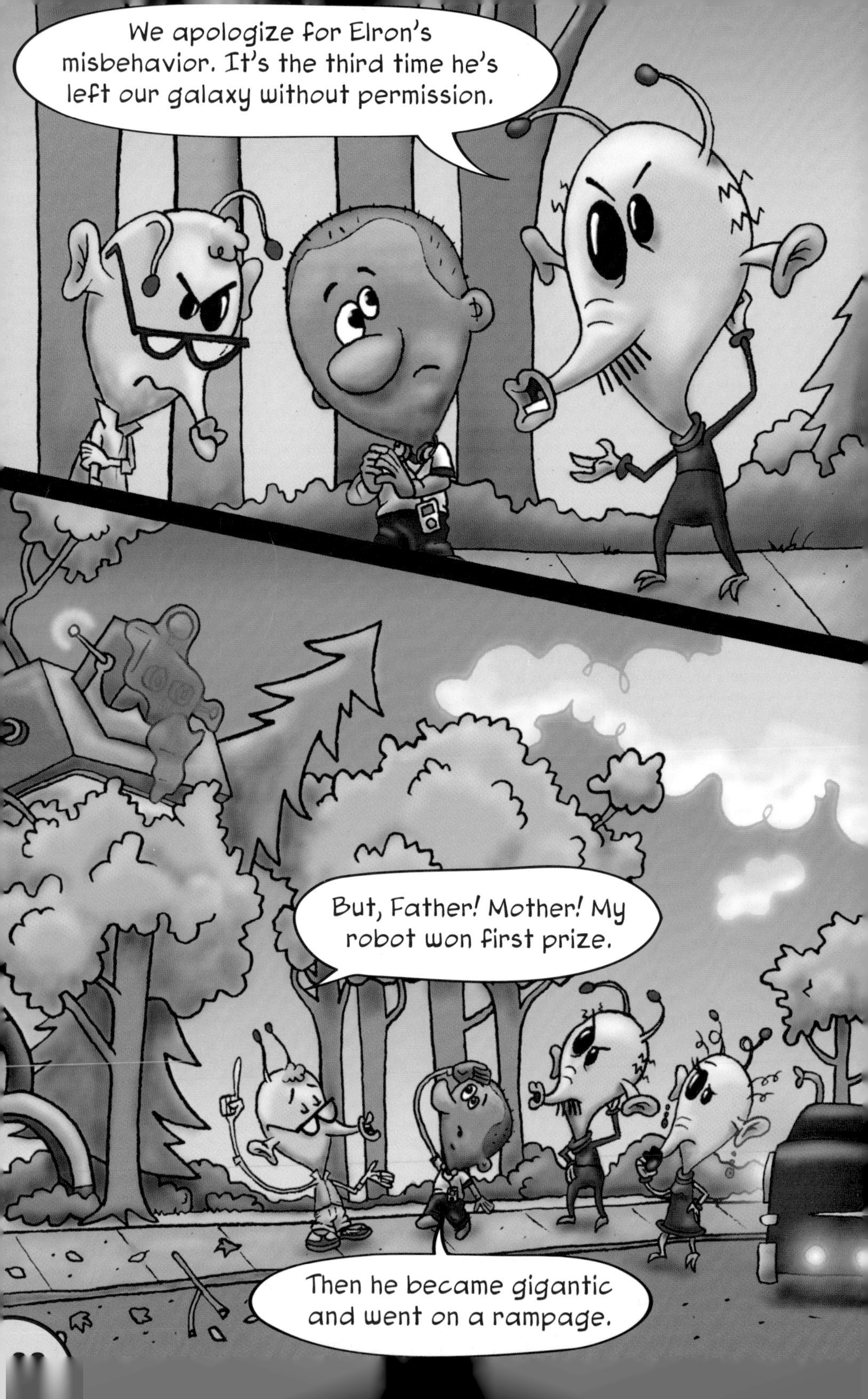
We apologize for Elron's misbehavior. It's the third time he's left our galaxy without permission.
But, Father! Mother! My robot won first prize.
Then he became gigantic and went on a rampage.

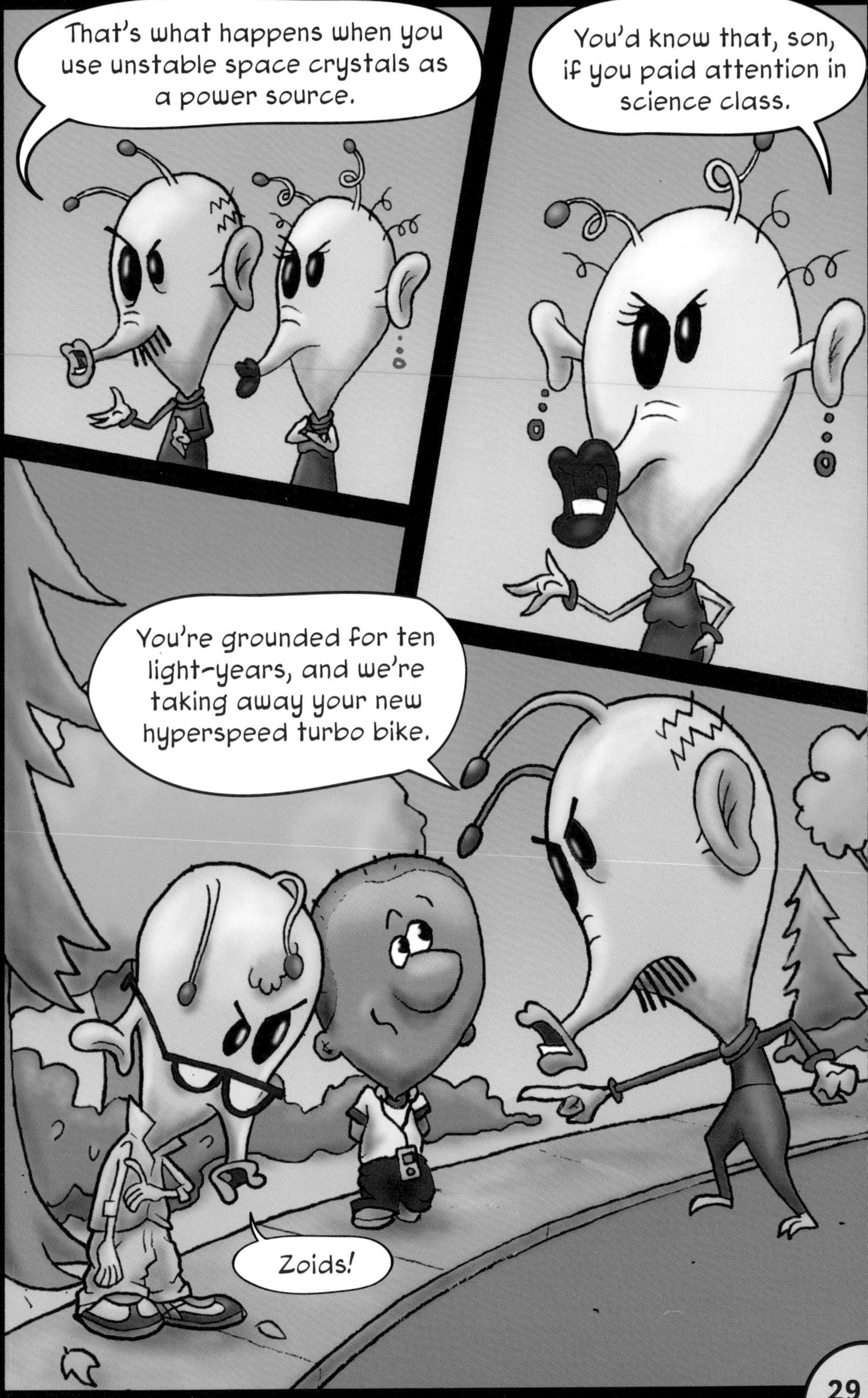
That's what happens when you use unstable space crystals as a power source.
You'd know that, son, if you paid attention in science class.
You're grounded for ten light-years, and we're taking away your new hyperspeed turbo bike.
Zoids!

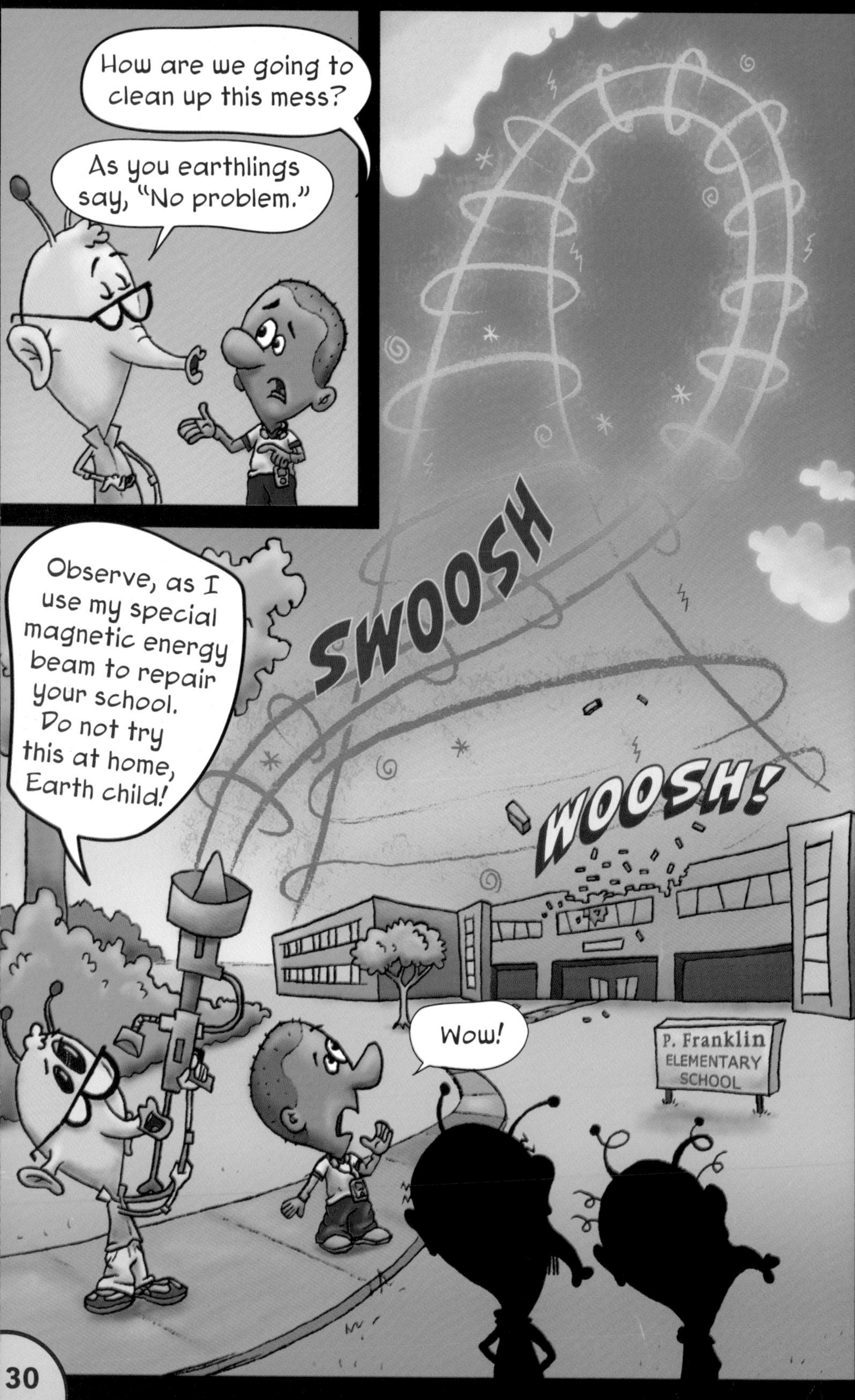
How are we going to clean up this mess?
As you earthlings say, "No problem."
Observe, as I use my special magnetic energy beam to repair your school. Do not try this at home, Earth child!
SWOOSH
WOOSH!
Wow!
P. Franklin ELEMENTARY SCHOOL

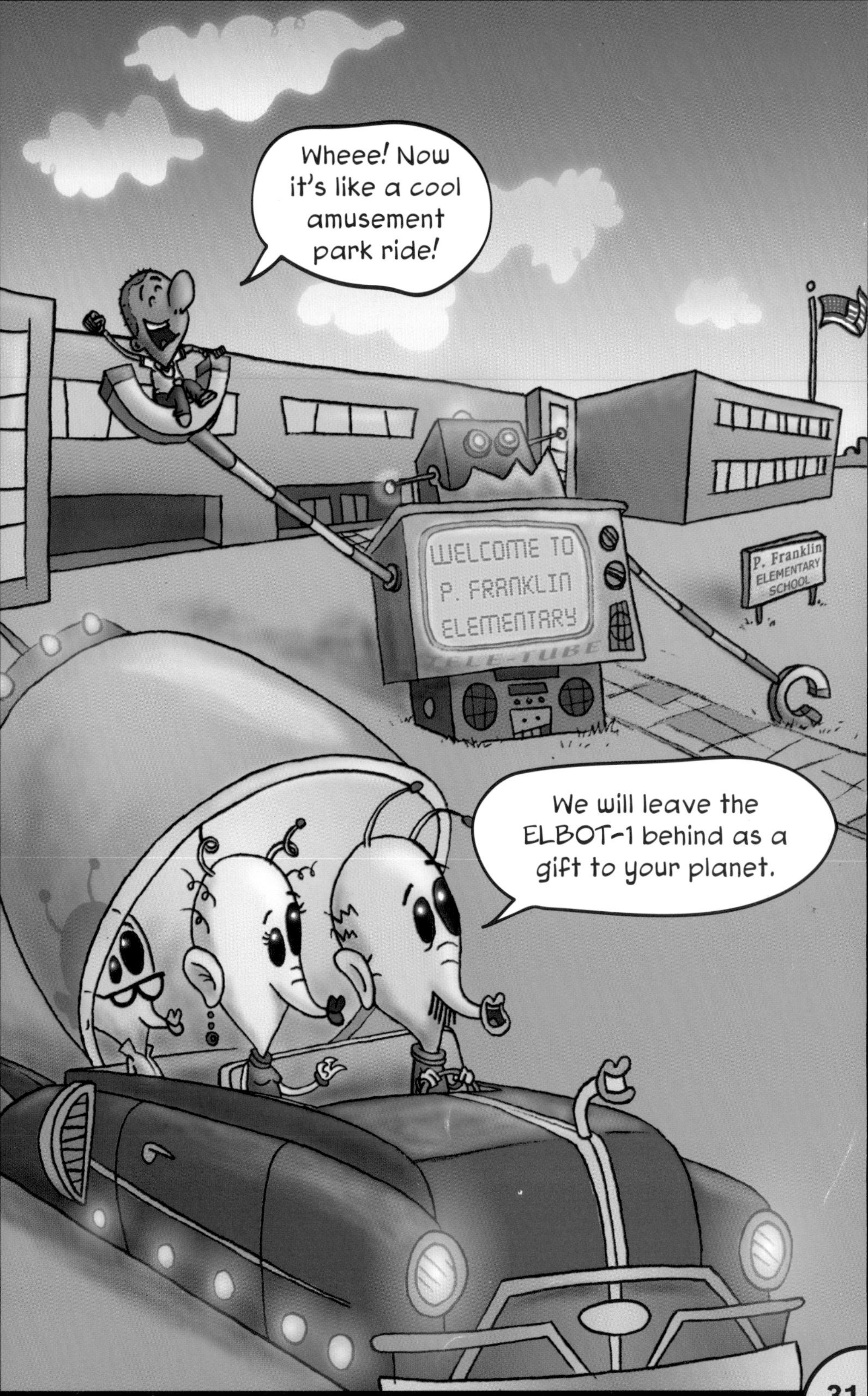
Wheee! Now it's like a cool amusement park ride!
WELCOME TO P. FRANKLIN ELEMENTARY
TELE-TUBE
P. Franklin ELEMENTARY SCHOOL
We will leave the ELBOT-1 behind as a gift to your planet.

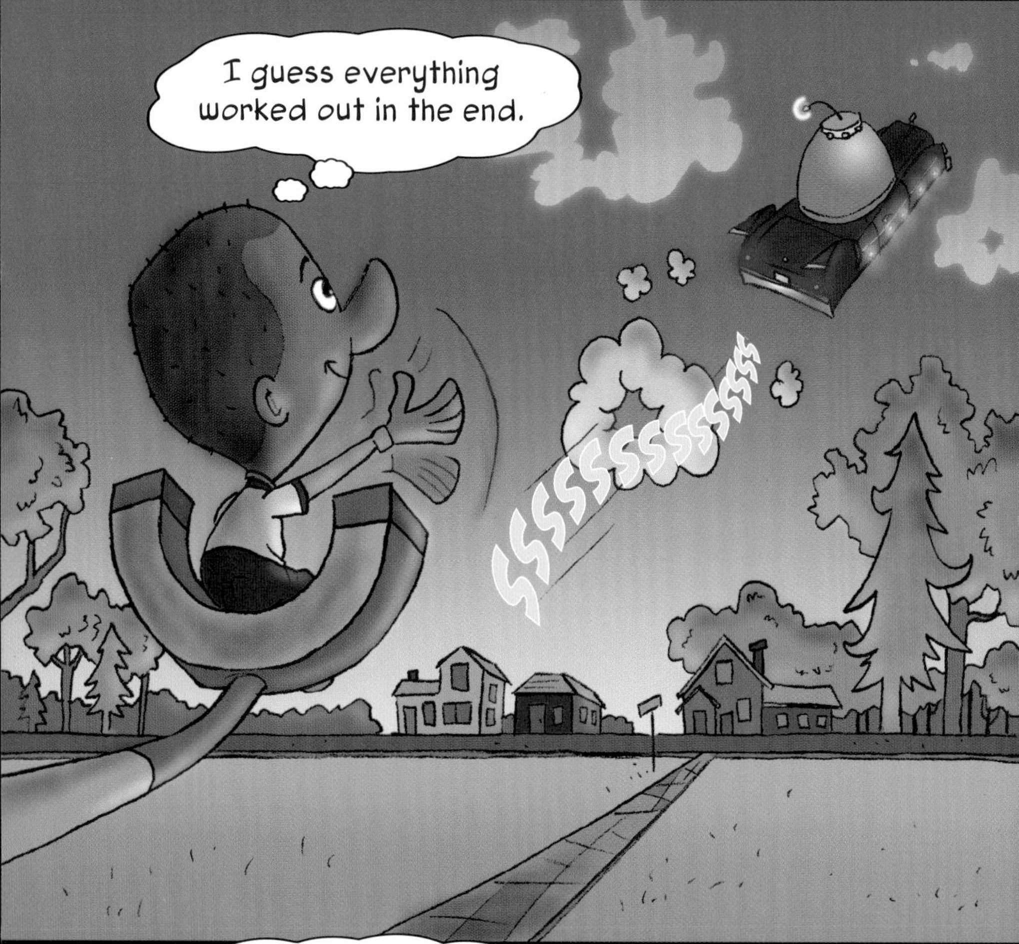
I guess everything worked out in the end.
SSSSSSSSSSSSSS

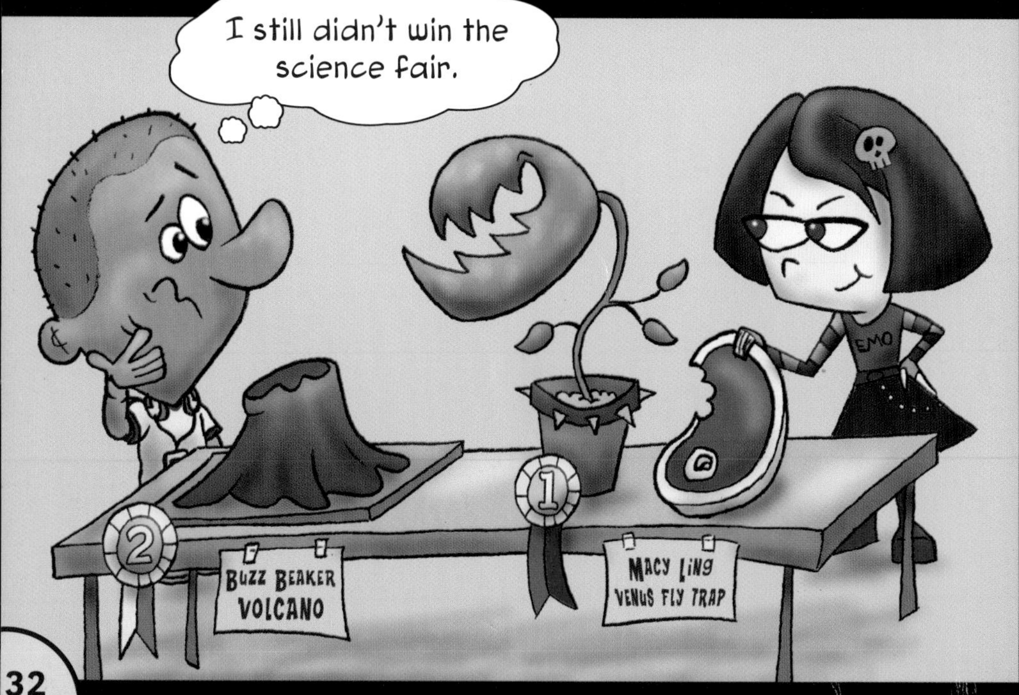
I still didn't win the science fair.
EMO
1
2
BUZZ BEAKER
VOLCANO
MACY LING
VENUS FLY TRAP

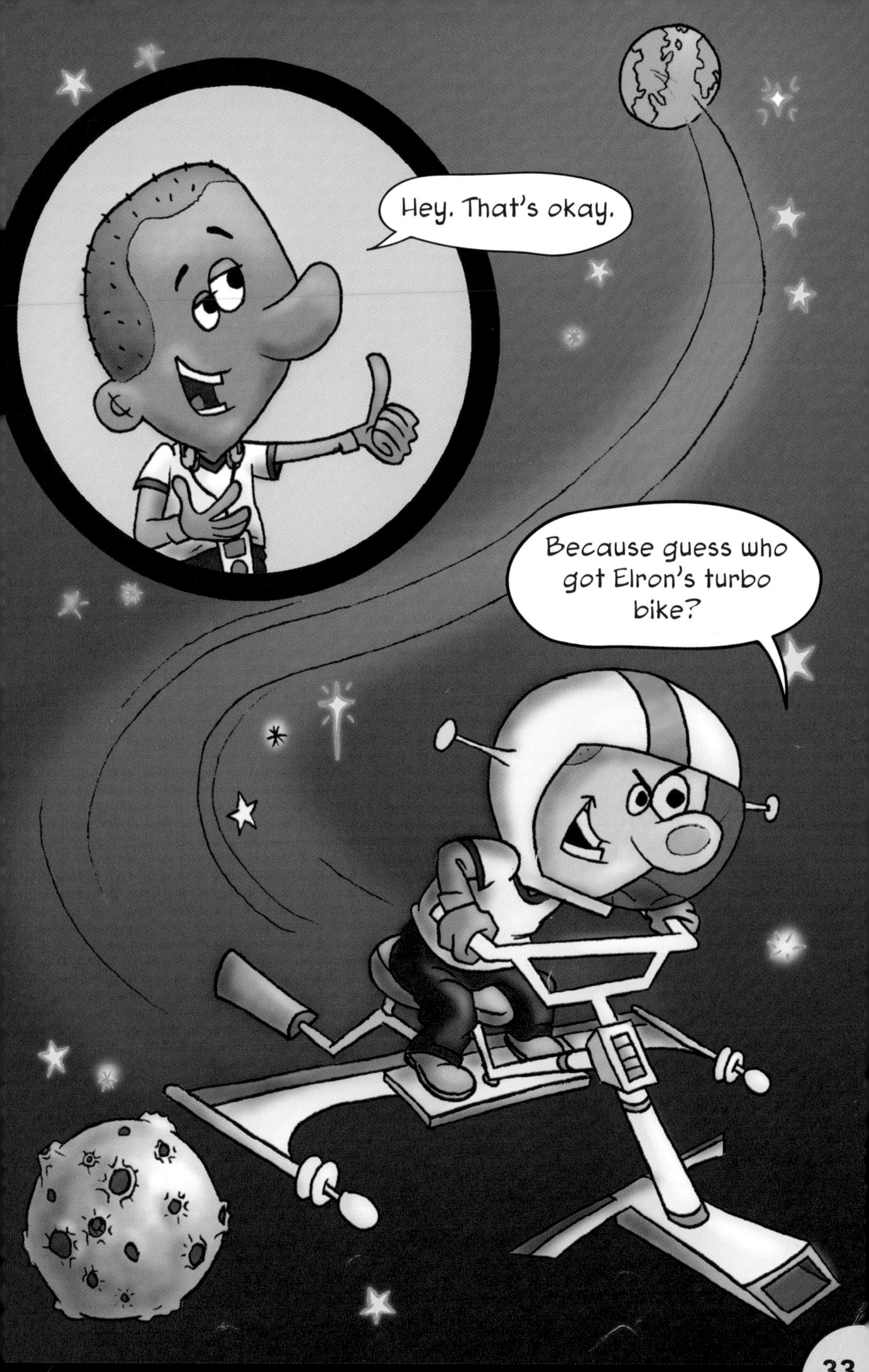
Hey. That's okay.
Because guess who got Elron's turbo bike?

ABOUT THE AUTHOR

Born in 1962 in Denver, Colorado, Scott Nickel works by day at Paws, Inc., Jim Davis's famous Garfield studio, and freelances by night. Burning the midnight oil, Scott has created hundreds of humorous greeting cards, and written several children's books, short fiction for *Boys' Life* magazine, comic strips, and lots of really funny knock-knock jokes. He has also eaten a lot of midnight snacks.

He was raised in Southern California, but in 1995 Scott moved to Indiana, where he currently lives with his wife, two sons, six cats, and several sea monkeys.

ABOUT THE ILLUSTRATOR

From a young age, Andy Smith knew he wanted to be an illustrator (if he couldn't be a space adventurer, superhero, or ghost hunter). After graduating from college in 1998, he began working at a handful of New York City animation studios on shows like *Courage the Cowardly Dog* and *Sheep in the Big City*, while also working in freelance illustration. Andy has since left New York City for Rochester, NY where he teaches high school art and illustration at the Rochester Institute of Technology.

GLOSSARY

barf (BARF)—the action of reversing a morning's breakfast for closer inspection. This usually happens when you are sick or nervous

foosh (FOOSH)—the sound of lava covering a science fair judge. (Also the sound of losing the first-place ribbon at a science fair!)

hyperspeed (HY-pur-SPEED)—faster than any vehicle found on Earth

rampage (RAM-payj)—if a person, or a robot, goes on a rampage, they race around, making lots of noise and destroying things

unstable (uhn-STAY-buhl)—not firm or steady

volcano (vol-KAY-noh)—a mountain with vents through which lava, ash, and cinders erupt. Volcanoes are found across the Earth's surface, or at science fairs.

zoids (ZOYDZ)—a word used by alien children when grounded by their parents. It does not mean "cool" or "wonderful."

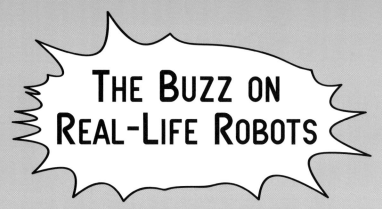

THE BUZZ ON REAL-LIFE ROBOTS

The world's first robot was named Elektro. He had a robot pet dog named Sparko. They appeared at the 1939 World's Fair in New York City. Elektro could say 77 words and move forward and backward.

The word "robot" comes from Czechoslovakia and means "servant."

What is the most difficult thing for a robot to do? Walk. Japanese inventors have made robots that can dance!

Over ninety percent of robots work in factories. They do everything from building cars to making computers.

Some robots are made for dangerous activities. Robug III was built in England and has eight legs. It was designed to enter sites that have such extreme radiation that a human could never survive them.

Underwater robots called "robo lobsters" creep along the rocky bottom of the sea. Their sensitive equipment can find explosive mines and other dangerous devices.

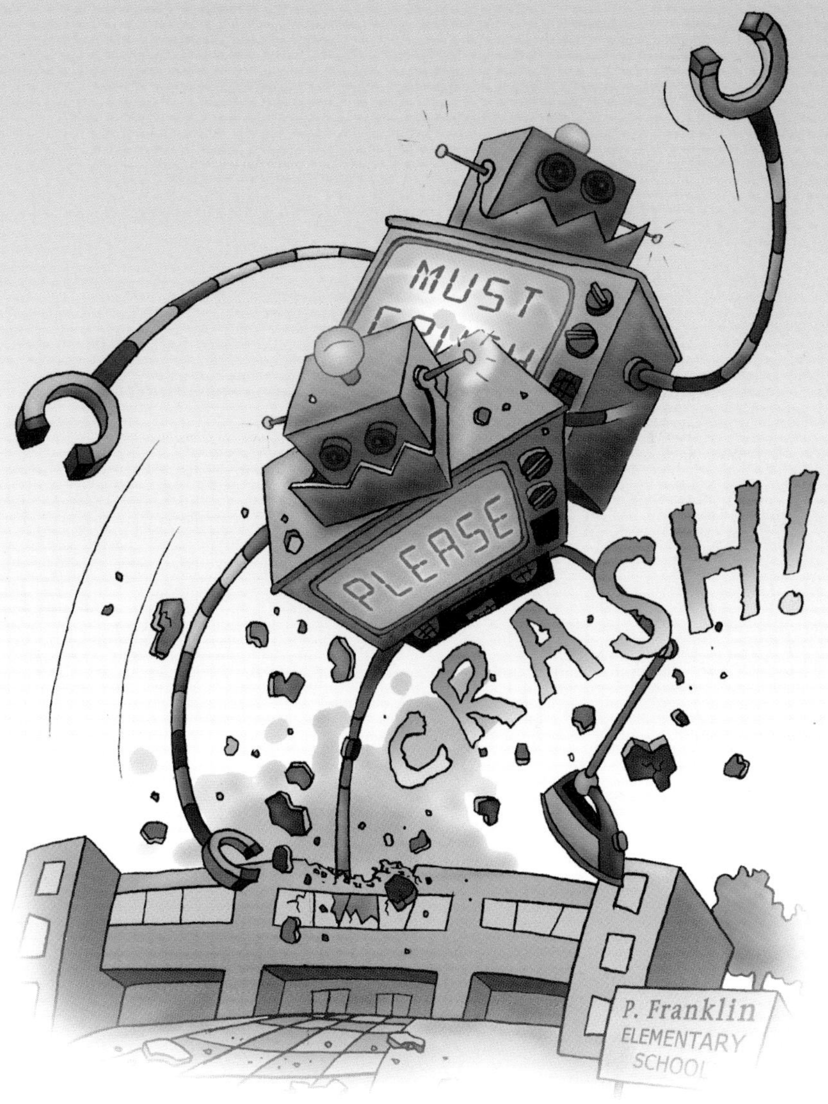
MUST
PLEASE
CRASH!
P. Franklin
ELEMENTARY
SCHOOL

DISCUSSION QUESTIONS

1. The main character of this book, Buzz, wants to win the science fair. Have you ever wanted to win a contest or fair? Why? How did you feel afterward, whether you won or not?

2. At what point in the story did you think that Elron might be different from the other students? What clues did the author give you?

3. If you had to face the same kind of danger Buzz did, how would you handle the giant escaped robot?

WRITING PROMPTS

1. Imagine the world's biggest school science fair. Now, imagine you can create anything you have ever wanted. Describe what you would make for the fair. Tell us how it works. Does your entry win a prize?

2. Parents find out when we do something wrong no matter if we live on a distant planet or here on Earth. Describe a time your parents found out about something you did wrong. How did they react and how did you feel when you were caught?

3. Buzz shows a lot of bravery for defending his town from Elbot-1. Tell about a time you were brave. What was the situation and how did you face it? Do you feel different about yourself when you are brave?

INTERNET SITES

Do you want to know more about subjects related to this book? Or are you interested in learning about other topics? Then check out FactHound, a fun, easy way to find Internet sites.

Our investigative staff has already sniffed out great sites for you!

Here's how to use FactHound:

1. Visit **www.facthound.com**

2. Select your grade level.

3. To learn more about subjects related to this book, type in the book's ISBN number: **1-59889-055-7**.

4. Click the **Fetch It** button.

FactHound will fetch the best Internet sites for you!

www.FactHound.com
_{SM}